Small Town Dreams
The Lives Of Teenagers

Angela Tibbs

Small Town Dreams

The Lives Of Teenagers

Bell Sheep Publishing

214 E. 10th Street

Georgetown, Illinois, 61846

bellpublishing17@gmail.com

(217)474-0410

Editions ISBNS;

Paperback; 979-8-9988008-0-1

E-book;   979-8-9988008-1-8

Hardback;   979-8-9906561-9-2

Table Of Contents

Chapter One

Lane's Senior Year

Austin, Lane, and Rosanna made it safely back to Georgetown after a long nine and half hour drive. After droppin Lane off at her parent's house Austin drove to his house, and as Austin and Rosanna got their stuff out of trunk the car Austin's father walked out onto the porch and said, "Rosanna, I didn't expect to see you with my son. When did he pick you up?"

"I was visitin Kelli in Saltillo, Mississippi, and ran into Austin at the local diner." Rosanna said, crackin a big smile. "So, I decided to come back with him to Illinois. You don't mind if I stay here do you?"

Austin's father thought for a minute and then replied, "Sure, I don't mind if you stay with us. Austin can show you around our little town since you haven't got to see yet, and I'm sure that he would love to have you see him perform at the fair. He has his own little fanbase and the girls just swoon all over him."

"Really?"

"Yes, Austin didn't tell you about that?"

"No." Rosanna replied, as she looked at Austin very surprised.

"Austin, didn't tell me about that when he had told he had played in the talent show."

"I think it was beginnin to upset Jessica because all these girls would come up to him wantin a picture or autograph. She didn't like that they were tryin to steal him away from her because she did find lots of telephone numbers in his jean pockets that one summer." Austin's father said, with a laugh as he watched the two walk into the house.

On a hot and muggy July Saturday mornin Austin, Rosanna, Brandon and Sophia were swimmin in the pool, Austin's parents were workin in the garden about five feet away. Around noon Austin and Rosanna went inside to get somethin to eat. As they walked into the dinin Rosanna saw the piano in the corner and said, "I didn't know that you had a piano."

"Yes, my parents have had it since I was very young." Austin said, as he put his towel on the piano bench so they could sit down. "I'm surprised you didn't see it when you came for Thanksgivin."

After sittin down on the piano bench Rosanna began to play it, and Austin was surprised because he didn't realize she knew how to play. As he watched her Austin said, "You are really good…"

"I had to take piano and dance lessons when I was younger." Rosanna said, as she looked at him. "My parents told me it would help me if I wanted to become an actor like them. My problem was I didn't want to practice my piano, but I loved to dance so I chose dance instead of music."

"I had the same problem with my guitar lessons I didn't want to practice either."

"Do you know this song." Rosanna said, as she started to play a song.

Austin listened to it tryin to figure it out, but he couldn't. He listened a little bit longer and said, "I don't know what song that is."

"Unforgettable in every way." Rosanna sang to him crackin a big smile. "And forevermore that's how you stay."

"That's why darlin it's incredible that's someone so unforgettable thinks that I am unforgettable too." Austin said, singin the next few lines in the song surprisin Rosanna's with his singin ability.

Next door Jaelyn had noticed that Austin's car was home, so she walked over from Hope's pool party to visit with Austin because he hadn't called to let her know that he was back in town. Jaelyn walked up onto the back porch and said, "Brandon, is your brother home?"

"Yea, he's inside." Brandon replied, as he walked around in the pool not givin it a second thought.

"I'm goin to go say hello." Jaelyn said, as she opened the back door and walked into the house.

As she walked into the kitchen she saw Austin sittin by the piano and singin, so she started to walk toward the dinnin room then saw the woman that was at his house on Thanksgivin. Jaelyn decided to stand in the doorway and just watch the two of them. She still had no idea what was goin on between them, but Jaelyn was goin to watch and find out.

"Unforgettable in every way and forevermore that's how you'll stay."

"That's why darlin it's incredible that someone so unforgettable." Austin and Rosanna sang together smilin at each other. "Thinks that I am unforgettable, too."

Rosanna played the last few notes and then said, "King, you knew that song."

"I know, once you started to sing the words I realized what song it was."

"How did you know all the words to it?" Rosanna said, with a big smile as she started to run her fingers through his hair.

"Jessica and I use to sing that song all the time." Austin explained, with sadness in his eyes.

"Oh..." Rosanna said, as she cracked a grin puttin her hand on his cheek. "It's too bad you have a girlfriend, Austin. I would love have that spot in your life."

"I need to call Jaelyn. I'm sure she's wonderin if I'm back in town or not."

"Actually, I know you're in town." Jaelyn yelled, from the doorway. "And I see that you are still hangin out with the girl who was here at Thanksgivin."

"Sweetness," Austin said, as he turned around and saw her standin in the doorway very upset him. "I was goin to call you."

"No you weren't."

"Yes, I was. I have just been a little busy."

"I'm sure you were." Jaelyn said, as she started to walk out of the kitchen and out the back door.

"Jaelyn, wait." Austin said, as he got up from the piano bench and ran through the kitchen and out the back door.

"You don't want me you want her."

"She is just a friend." Austin said, as he grabbed her arm in front of the gazebo. "Will you please stop and talk to me."

Jaelyn didn't say anything she just started to cry as she put her head into Austin's chest. Makin a scene in front of everyone on purpose because she wanted the girls at the party to see that Austin and her were fightin like a datin couple.

Across the yard Reese, Jaedyn, Hope, and all the other guests at Hope's party were watchin the drama unfold with Austin and Jaelyn. Jaedyn was very upset that Austin was makin her sister cry and she was goin to have to teach him a lesson for doin it. Reese was confused about why Jaelyn and Austin were fightin like a datin couple when they were just friends. Standin at the back door Rosanna watched Austin and Jaelyn jealous that Austin wanted to be with Jaelyn.

"You are lyin to me?" Jaelyn asked, lookin at him with fear in her green eyes.

"I'm not lyin to you." Austin said, crackin his boyish grin.

"Rosanna and I ran into each other down in Mississippi when Lane and I went down there. She just came back with me because she was bored in Mississippi."

"And this place is any better?"

"I know, I'm goin to show her around town."

"Austin." Jaelyn said, as she wiped her eyes. "Is that all?."

"Yes." Austin said, as he ran his hand up and down her back.

Jaelyn cracked a little devilish grin as she leaned over and gave him a kiss as she put her arms around him. Across the yard Reese was still watchin everythin, and gettin very upset with what she was seein. Reese didn't understand Austin and Jaelyn's connection, and why they were so close. Reese was still determined to make Austin her boyfriend no matter what it took to get him.

Down here in Saltillo, Mississippi, I was still workin at diner almost every day. Christine, Beverly, Lee Ann, and Eloise were enjoyin their summer still as they spent many of their days at dance class, practicin their instruments, singin, and buyin outfits that they didn't really need to buy. I was surprised when Eloise broke up with me not long after Austin left,. and she told me that she needed to focus on her dancin to get into Julliard. I was a little upset at first because even though I was messin around with Lee Ann I still wanted to be with Eloise.

On a hot muggy Friday afternoon Lee Ann, Beverly, Christine, and Eloise were at the diner eatin lunch when Eloise took a bite of her french fry covered in ketchup she smiled and asked, "Did any of you girls get Austin Reid's number?"

"Why are you askin?" Lee Ann asked, crackin a big smile as she took a drink of her milkshake.

"I think he's kinda of cute."

"Do you like him?" Beverly asked, with a big smile as she looked at Eloise.

"Yes, I do."

"Maybe Larlee has his phone number and she can give it to you." Christine said, as she took a drink of her milkshake.

"Hopefully, she does." Eloise replied, very excited as she ate another fry.

All the girls laughed before they finished eatin their lunch. Before they left Eloise talked to Larlee about gettin Austin's number. Larlee told her that she would need a few days because she would need to talk to her great niece to get it for her. A few days Larlee called Lane to get Austin's number for Eloise, and explained to Lane why she was askin for it.

On Sunday mornin in Illinois Austin and the rest of his family made it to church about ten minutes before it started. As the family walked into the church, everyone standin in the lobby couldn't believe that Rosanna Aydelotte was in their church. Many of the people in the congregation walked up to Rosanna and asked her for an autograph. Rosanna wasn't happy that people were crowdin her when she was hangin out with her friends. Hope, Reese, Peyton, Maddy, and a few other girls were standin up against the wall just watchin what was goin on. The girls were surprised when Jaelyn didn't walk over to where Austin was to say hello to him, but Jaelyn did have a big smile, and her eyes lit up as she looked at him.

The Reid family made their way to the pew they set in every Sunday mornin, and as they set down Jessica's mother looked over at Austin. She saw a familiar look of sadness in his eyes, and after Austin sat down beside her in the pew she looked at him and said, "Austin, are you doin all right?"

"I'm doin all right, Mrs. Roth." Austin replied, crackin his boyish smile. "I was wonderin if I can come over and visit one day."

"Austin, you know that you can come over anytime to visit."

"Ok, I just wanted to make sure it was all right."

"So did you have a good time this summer when you and Lane went on your trip to Mississippi?"

"Yes, we did."

"Anything happen while you were down there?" Jessica's mother asked, makin conversation.

"No, not that I can think of." Austin replied, as he looked up at the choir and saw Jaelyn smilin at him.

The music started to play and the choir sarted to sing the mornin hymns. After they were sung the preacher walked up to the podium, and as he looked down at his bible he said,

"Matthew 5: 27, and when you find it say amen."

Within a few minutes a lot of scattered amens went through the crowd, and Rosanna was a little confused why the preacher was havin the congregation do it. She saw the congregation openin their bibles and turnin to the page in the scripture, and sayin amen once they had found it.

"Today, we are goin to talk about lust." The preacher said, as he looked up at the congregation. "It's not right for a man and woman to be together sexually until they are married. I know the kids today think that it's all right to partake in what everybody else doin, but kids let me tell you that it's not god's way. You are to be clean vessels of the lord, so that you can do good in this world. The devil will take you down if you give in and give him just a crack to get into your life."

"Preach it!" A grey-haired older gentleman said, yelled from the back row.

"In Matthew five Jesus says you have heard that it was said you shall not commit adultery. But I say to you that everyone who looks at woman with lustful intent has already committed adultery with her in his heart. If your right eye causes you to sin; tear it out and throw it away. For it is better that you lose one of your members than that your whole body be thrown into hell. And if your right hand causes you to sin, cut it off and throw it away. For it is better that you lose one of your members than that your whole body go into hell."

"That's right, tell them." An overly plump woman with very red hair said, settin in the front row.

"Tell them what disobedience will do."

"If you do start havin sex you'll be caught up in that vice, and you will not get the inheritance of God." The preacher said, with a big smile as he looked at his congregation very seriously. "Because you will be in rebellion and disobedience of god's word."

Rosanna had grown up catholic, and the way this preacher was preachin the words he was sayin affected her in a way that she wasn't . expectin She was feelin convicted about the way she lived her life but was it enough to convince her to stop. She had never saw preachin the way the the preacher preached his sermon.

While Austin was sittin in church, Lane was just wakin up from the night before. Lane's father hadn't been to church in years, so Lane didn't have to worry about gettin up early every Sunday to go to church. Every now and again Lane did go with her one set of grandparents, and she had begun to watch preachers on television. The lord had begun doin a work in her that would change her life in ways that she hadn't seen yet. Lane didn't know what the lord had called her to do, but she knew that it would be something that would not only change her life but also the lives of others.

Back at the church the preacher had gotten back to message, and he was preachin with hellfire and brimstone. He was yellin and pointin at the congregation which had some of them a little scared because he had never preached that way to them. As he wiped his brow with his handkerchief the preacher said, "With this world passin away and humans pershin it's shameful that a person's purpose isn't fulfilled because he or she has turned from God to fulfill the lust of the flesh. Don't be that stupid. Find your purpose on the earth and fulfill it, so that you will hear the lord say well done my good and faithful servant."

In my own life, I was at church every Sunday because my mother wanted us to be there. I was usually bored by the sermons because nothin the preacher preached caught my attention. Although I know that I should have listened closer to a few of them because I was turnin away from the lord as I enjoyed the taste of liquor and with the flesh of the opposite sex. Usually, every Sunday at church Eloise would look over at Lee Ann and I but then look away like she didn't care about us bein together. I don't know maybe she was second guessin her decision to break up with me.

Back in Illinois, the preacher was comin to the end of his sermon. Many people were listenin to the preacher was sayin, and there was a lot of young people who were taken in every word. As he turned in his bible he said, "In closin, I only ask you this. Please turn away from lust and do not let it take you down a road that will destroy you in the end. God has a good life for you, but you have to turn away from sin and follow Jesus with all your heart. "

"Preach it." The greyed haired man yelled, from the back row.

"Lord, I ask that what was talked about today in this buildin is brought back to every person that's here today. When they come to a situation, and they have to make a decision I ask that you help them make the right choice. Let your light shine through those who walked through the door today. I ask this in Jesus name, amen and amen."

That afternoon Austin and Rosanna were lyin on Rosanna bed takin a nap when Rosanna started pressin on Austin's nose, then on his mouth, and then blew in his ear because he was asleep. After about five minutes Austin opened his eyes, looked over at her, and said, "Why are you doin that?"

"I want to see those blue eyes of yours." Rosanna replied, crackin a big smile as she leaned on her arm lookin up at him.

"I lied to Jaelyn and told her you and I are just friends." Austin explained, as he stared into her blue green eyes.

"How did you lie to her? We are friends."

"I didn't tell her the truth that you and I have slept together."

"Well, I wouldn't tell her that." Rosanna explained, as she snuggled up against his shoulder.

"Why not?" Austin said, as he looked back up at the cecilin.

"She will hate your guts and want nothin to do with you after that."

"You think so?"

"King," Rosanna said, as she lifted up her head to look into his eyes.

"I'm a woman and if my man did that to me I would hate him, and I definitely wouldn't want anymore to do with him."

"Ok, Sweetkins. I won't tell her about us.."

"Good!." Rosanna said, crackin a little grin as she kissed him on the cheek

The third week of July Lane had her surgery, and the doctors broke her top jaw broke movin it up. She stayed in the hospital for a few days before she could finally go home. The doctors told her it would be best if she didn't talk because it would help her recover faster. Lane didn't like to take orders and she started to sing with the radio. The doctors did tell her that there were screws and plates in mouth, and that she could go back in for surgery to have them taken out.

On a hot and muggy Friday mornin Austin and Rosanna decided to go fishin at the local damn just outside of town. After they found a spot close to the water Austin asked, "So are you goin to put the worm on your hook before you throw it into the water?"

"Eww!" Rosanna said, with the most digustin look on her face as she thought about it. "No, you are goin to do it,"

"Ok." Austin said, as he opened the worm container and put the worm on her fishpole hook.

Austin then gave the pole to Rosanna and then helped her cast the line into the water. Austin then baited his hook, cast his pole, he took his spot on the dirt and waited for the fish to bite. Austin could tell that Rosanna didn't like waitin on the fish because she started makin phone calls to her manager.

She was in the middle of her phone call with her manager when her pole moved, but she didn't know what to do. Austin grabbed the pole and started reelin it in as he watched Rosanna stay on the phone talkin to her manager as Austin reeled the fish in, took it off the hook, and threw it back into the water.

By that afternoon Rosanna had gotten the hang of reelin fish in, and she had caught more fish than Austin. Austin still had to bait the hook and take the fish off the hook, but the two were havin fun together.

As the sun started to go down, Austin and Rosanna began to pack up their gear and walk back to the car. Rosanna got in the passenger seat while Austin put stuff in the trunk. Rosanna looked at the picture of Jessica, and she wondered if Austin had found any of the things the little girl told him about. As she looked back at Austin, and then the picture again she said, "Jessica, I sure hope you are back on the earth again to give Austin a a reason for livin because he lost his reason to live the day you were taken away from him that September afternoon."

Austin drove home from the dam into the driveway, parked the car, and as he got into the trunk to get the fishin poles and tackle box out of it he noticed Hope and Eileen watchin him from Hope's front porch. Austin waved and smiled but neither one waved back at him, so Austin took the stuff in the garage as Rosanna made her way into the house. Austin walked out of the garage, and still saw Hope and Elieen settin on to porch swing watchin him. Austin looked at his car and thought about what the little girl had said about the letter bein the glovebox of the car. He had been puttin it off for so long, and he decided it was time to find out for sure if there was a letter in there. Austin walked over to the car and got into the passenger side which Elieen and Hope thought was a little weird. He took a deep breath, opened the glovebox, and started to pull out what was in it. As he started to put things away he found a folded up piece of paper, and as he took a deep breath he opened it to find a letter from Jessica to him.

The letter read;

Dear Austin,

If you are readin this it means that I am on an air force base some-where in this country or abroad. I know that you will be gettin your license soon and will be able to drive where you want to go. I know that your father isn't goin to give you a car to drive after you get them, and I know my father would rather my car stay in the garage where he can drive now and then, but I've told him to give it to you so you'll .have a piece of me with you while I'm away. Then when I come home we can make more memories in it. Please take good care of my car and don't wreck it because I will have to hurt you.

Love Always,

Jessica

Austin eyes filled up with tears as he read love always Jessica because he knew without a doubt that she had written the letter to him. He knew that Jessica wanted him to have a piece of her while she was makin her way in the air force. He felt so ashamed about what he had done

with Rosanna, and what might happen with Jaelyn if he let the relationship grow into the relationship Jessica told him it would be. Austin sat in
the car for a good hour to make sure all of his tears were out, and he could
walk into the house so that his parents wouldn't know that anything was
wrong with him. Austin walked into the house, and made his way to the
kitchen where a plate of food from supper was waitin on him. Austin had
put his plate in the microwave, and he was leanin up against the
cabinets when Rosanna walked into the kitchen and said, "Austin, is
everything all right?"

"Yea." Austin said, still wipin tears from his eyes.

As she walked over and put her arms around his neck Rosanna said,
"Austin, what is botherin you?"

"I looked in the glovebox of the car." Austin replied, as he looked into her blue green eyes

"What did you find?." Rosanna said, seein both fear and sadness in his eyes.

"I found the letter the little girl said that she wrote."

"The letter that Jessica wrote about you gettin the car when she's in the air force?"

"Yes, that letter.."

"No, damn way?" Rosanna said, not believin a word of what Austin was tellin her.

"Yes, I found it." Austin said, as tears started to fall from his eyes.

"That's why it took me an hour to come inside the house."

"I want to see it."

"Can I show it to you tomorrow because I'm still a little overwhelmed by what I found. Not to mention I need to wrap my head around the possibility Jessica is alive and livin again."

"Yes, of course. This may change my mind on reincarnation if you find everything she told you find."

"I think I'm goin to need a drink." Austin said, with a laugh as he wiped the tears from his eyes.

"It's all right. I have some vodka and bourbon in my bag." Rosanna said, with a little laugh as she ran her fingers through the back of his hair.

The next mornin after eatin breakfast and gettin awake Austin and Rosanna went out to his car, and he got the letter out of the glove box showin it to her. Rosanna was stunned that the little girl in Missi-ssippi would know about a letter a teenage girl had written. She could tell by the look on Austin's face that he was still in shock, Rosanna also noticed group of girls settin on the porch next door, and there were about six of them.

Rosanna made sure that Jaelyn wasn't settin on the porch before she leaned over and gave Austin a very passionate kiss.

"What was that for?" Austin asked, after the kiss was over with the funniest look on his face.

"Your nosy neighbors." Rosanna said, with a big smile as she looked over at them.

Austin looked over at the porch and saw Jaedyn there with the rest of the girls, and he knew that he would be in trouble with Jaelyn because of Jaedyn. After Rosanna had put the letter back in the glove box he said, "Well, Jaelyn isn't goin to talk to me because her big sister is over there, and she doesn't look very happy."

"Sorry." Rosanna said, with a big smile on her face and a laugh. "I'm sure you can smooth it over you just have to sweet talk Jaelyn like you did the other day."

"Really?"

"Yes."

"You think this is funny?" Austin said, gettin a little upset with Rosanna because she liked to get him in trouble with Jaelyn.

"Yes, I do." Rosanna said, with a big laugh and smile as she leaned her head back against the head rest of the seat.

At the end of July Austin had taken Rosanna out to Forest Glenn to walk the trails. Austin told Rosanna about all the different trails they would walk durin the year, and how they made it an adventure to get to the end of the trail and back to the car. Austin explained also about the serious talks the two would have about what life was goin to be like for them once they were grown, and how they were goin to change the world in their own way. When the Austin walked the trail down to the river after Jessica's death he told Rosanna that he always got a strange feelin when walkin by the tower, and Austin thought that he could feel Jessica walkin beside him when he was out there.. Austin decided to take her to other places in town that were important to the two of them. They went to the local park where Austin played baseball in the summer league, and Jessica would be there to cheer him on along with a few others. Then to the grade school, Frasier school, the junior high, and the high school. The two set on the bleachers and Austin explained about the homecomin week games, and that he has played on the field the entire time he's been in high school.

Last, he told her how he and Jessica would watch the sunset from her front porch or his settin in the swing, and how they loved to watch the thunderstorms roll through settin on the swing covered up with a blanket.

It was a stormy rainy night. Austin and Rosanna had gone to bed around ten, and the two of them were in dreamland, Austin turned over in the bed and in his dream he saw Jessica settin on the bed beside him. As he looked at her, she put her hand on his and said, "Sunshine, you found my letter didn't you?"

"Yes, I found the letter.." Austin replied, as he looked up at her with fear in his eyes.

"You know that I'm alive and a little girl again in this world."

"Yes, but now what am I supposed to do?"

"Live your life and become the star that you're meant to."

"Who am I supposed to love until you grow up?" Austin asked, with a confused look.

"You are supposed to fall in love with Jaelyn."

"Really? I thought it was supposed to be Rosanna."

"Yes, really. I hate the thought of you bein with her, but there are lessons to be learned while you're with her.."

29

"Ok, Satnin." Austin replied, with sadness in his eyes and on his face

Austin talked with Jessica in his dream for what seemed to be a long time. Around two o' clock in the mornin Austin woke up in a cold sweat, so he grabbed a book out of the nightstand drawer and made his way downstairs to the kitchen. After gettin a late-night snack and some milk, Austin set down at the kitchen table and started to look through the book. As Austin looked through the pictures and the things he and Jessica had written, he started to cry because he missed her so much even though he knew a new truth. There was trouble between his heart and his head because of what he had learned in church that when it's our time to go we leave our bodies we go to God. Now knowin that Jessica is on the earth again in a new body, and that we don't just live one life but many lives on the earth. Austin then thought about his relationship with Jaelyn, and how it would be affected once she found out that Jessica was alive again. Questions raged in his head; How can I love Jaelyn knowin I'm only goin to hurt her? Will I love Jaelyn more than Jessica and hurt Jessica down the road? Will I hurt Jaelyn to be with Jessica when she's old enough?

On Saturday mornin Rosanna went down for her mornin coffee, and she found Austin's mother in the kitchen makin breakfast. As she poured her coffee Austin's mother asked, "How did you sleep last night?"

"I slept all right, I guess." Rosanna replied, as she took that first sip.

"I heard Austin took you to all of his and Jessica's hang outs around town."

"Yes, he did. Do you think that he will ever find that love again with some-one else?"

"I don't think he will find love like that again.." Austin's mother said, as she walked over to the kitchen table. "The only way that would happen would be if Jessica comes back to the earth again, but I don't think that will happen any-time soon."

"Really? You don't?"

"I believe what the bible says that we live one life and then we go to be with Jesus for forever."

"Really? I'm startin to change my mind because with the internet there have been some stories about how Elvis Presley looked like a king from Turkey, and Michael Jackson looks like a pharaoh from Egypt or somethin like that."

"I wouldn't place much stock into that because it probably isn't true."

The two women sat down at the kitchen table after Austin's mother got done with the last few pancakes. Settin on the table was a scrapbook with a picture of Austin and Jessica on the front of it from when they were young children. In the photo slot on top of the scrapbook was a picture of Jessica and Austin huggin each other, Jessica was huggin Austin so tight around the neck with a big smile on her face, and Austin had the look of help me on his face because he couldn't really breathe because she was huggin him so tight.

As she looked at the book Rosanna asked, "What's this?"

Austin 's mother moved the book over closer to her, opened it, and said, "Oh, this is the scrapbook Austin and Jessica started in nineteen ninety to show their lives together through the years. They were goin to put important events in their lives separately and together as they went through life together."

"So where did they start at?"

"They put baby pictures in and picked out pictures of when they were young. There is a picture of Austin with his guitar that he got for Christmas."

Rosanna looked and the guitar was bigger than him when he got it because Austin was so small at the time. Then she looked at the next picture and it was a picture of Austin playin and singin to Jessica. Rosanna looked over at the next page and saw a picture of Austin and Jessica sittin on a porch swing. The next picture down was a picture of Jessica holdin up a picture of a fighter jet and the caption under it read "I'm goin to fly this when I'm out of school."

Austin's mother looked at the pictures and started to cry because she remembered how happy and in love Austin and Jessica were when those pictures were taken. Then she turned the page and there was a picture at Jessica and Austin sittin on the piano bench in their Halloween customs. Jessica was a fighter pilot and Austin was dressed up like Elvis Presley. Lookin at the picture Rosanna laughed and said, "Austin, does have an Elvis Presley obsession."

"Yes, he does." Austin's mother said, with a big laugh. "But that can be blamed on his cousin Lane because she went down to Graceland with a friend and brought him back a pair of sunglasses like Elvis used to wear.

The two of them started learnin about Elvis together ever since. They both want to be big stars someday and perform on the Georgetown Fair stage as the main act. But right now it seems that they are both chasin different dreams. "

"What do you mean?"

"Lane has this obsession of writin right now and is not learnin to play her guitar or sing. Austin has gotten more into movie and television than learnin his guitar and singin."

"Yes, Austin told me that he hadn't really sang since Jessica died." Rosanna replied, as she took a sip of coffee.

"I'm hopin that one day he will chase his dream to sing again because he was always so good when he sang in the talent show at the Georgetown Fair."

Austin's mother turned the page, and then there were two pages filled with Austin and Jessica at the fairgrounds at the Georgetown Fair. The caption on both pages were "Havin a blast at the Georgetown Fair." The pictures ranged from when they were small to the time they went to the fair in nineteen ninety-three. Turnin the page Austin's mother was a little curious about the next page because it didn't have any pictures just the caption "We're engaged!" Then she turned to the next page and found somethin that she wasn't expectin. The Caption on the page was "Our Weddin", and there was a piece of paper on one page with stained tear-drops. Austin's mother and Rosanna both looked at each other a little shocked by what they saw, so they started to read was on the piece of paper. It read;

Our Vows For Our Weddin Day

Austin, I, Jessica, take you as my husband. I will help you become the biggest star in the world and be your biggest fan at the same time. I know that the four years between us has made our love wait until we were both old enough to know what love really is. I adore you, sunshine. You are my world and my life revolves around only you. I know that life together won't be easy as we try to make both of our dreams come true as we work together as a team to make happen.

We can show this town that we can make it to forever just by lovin each other so much not lookin at the odds against us. I can't wait to walk the red carpet with you as you show me off to the world, and all the women of the world will have to be jealous of me because I'm the one who has your heart. I also can't wait to start a family with you and be the mother of your children. I hope that we will settle down in this town again to raise our family together while we fly to Hollywood only to show your incredible talent off to world. Sunshine, I can't wait to be your wife and love you forever

Jessica, I, Austin, take you as my wife. I will help you make your dreams come true as you fly high in the sky doin what you've always wanted to do since you were in fifth grade. Life will not always goin be easy for us because just like we saw our parents we will probably fight over stupid and silly things. I know that we will work through whatever problem that comes our way, but since we are both stubborn as mules it may take a long time. I will take care of you for the rest of our lives because you are my world. My life begins and ends with you.

Satnin. I can't wait to walk down the red carpet with you when
I have my first movie premiere in Hollywoodland. I love you, Satnin,
I can't wait to be your husband.

"I didn't know that they had done this." Austin's mother said, as she finished readin that last of Austin's vows.

"Hard to believe that they had their lives planned out at such a young age." Rosanna said, amazed that Austin and Jessica were so committed to each other.

"I didn't realize just how in love and committed the two of them were to each other."

"They were really childhood sweethearts?"

"Yes, they were." Austin's mother said, as she turned the page to look at the next page.

Just then Austin walked into the kitchen and saw Rosanna and his mother sittin at the table, and as he got a cup of coffee Austin said, "What are you two lookin at?"

"This book that was on the table." Austin's mother explained, as she looked over at him.

"I forgot to take that upstairs with me after I came down to eat a snack."

"When did the two of you start this?" Rosanna asked, as she looked up at him.

"In nineteen ninety." Austin replied, as he walked over and sat down at the table with them.

"Do you have any plans today, son?"

"Just hang out around here, I think. Rosanna is wantin to get some pool time in. I really do need to go over and see Jaelyn, so I might do that after I take my walk."

"You are goin to take a walk?"

"Yes, mother."

"Why do you seem surprised?" Rosanna asked, with a giggle.

"He doesn't normally take walks." Austin's mother replied, as she looked at her son.

"Well, today I am.." Austin said, as he finished his coffee, put it in the sink, and made his way out of the kitchen.

Austin's mother and Rosanna laughed as he walked out the front door because neither one understood why Austin was takin a walk. The two women finished lookin at the scrapbook, and still couldn't get over Austin and Jessica's commitment to each other at such a young age. The two spent a Good two hours talkin about what life would be like if Jessica had lived.

After Austin walked down the road and started walkin back toward the house, he decided to go and visit the Roth family. He had only seen them at church and hadn't really visited with them over the last year. As he walked up the driveway he saw Jessica's mother sittin on the porch swing watchin the traffic go by, and when he stepped onto the porch he said, "Mrs. Roth, how are you today?"

With a big smile she looked over at him and said, "I'm doin well, Austin. How about you?"

"I'm doin all right." Austin said, as he walked over and sat down on the porch swing beside her. "I can't complain.."

"How are you and that girl Rosanna gettin along?"

"All right, I guess."

"Are you playin at the Georgetown Fair talent show this year?"

"I think so." Austin said, crackin his boyish grin. "I'm thinkin about doin a duet with someone."

"That will be nice to see." Mrs. Roth said, with a big grin. "Is it goin to be with Rosanna?'

"No, it's goin to be with a girl who lives here in town."

"Anyone I know?"

"Yes, but you can't tell anyone if I tell you who it is."

"I won't tell a soul." Mrs. Roth said, with a big smile and laugh.

"Ok." Austin replied. "I'm doin a duet with Jaelyn Somerled."

"How sweet. You know that she has had a crush on you for the longest time."

"Really? I didn't know that." Austin said, crackin a little grin..

"I think she would be the perfect girl for you to go out with."

"Really?"

"I know that in your heart she will never replace my daughter." Mr. Roth explained. "But she would be a good girl to move forward with because she has an essence like Jessica that will keep you on your toes."

"No doubt about that." Austin replied, with a laugh surprised Mrs. Roth would give him the ok to be with someone else.

Two hours later Austin and Mrs. Roth reminisced about the old days, and Austin asked her if he could go to Jessica's room and just sit in there for a while. Mrs. Roth had no objection to him doin that, so Austin made his way to the front door and walked inside the house. As Austin made his way down the hall to Jessica's room he thought about all the times they had run down the hall to her room playin tag. Austin opened the bedroom door and stood there for a moment before he walked in. As he sat down on the bed and looked around the room, he took in the smell of her perfume and every memory he had in that room with her, When Austin laid down on the bed and looked up at the ceilin at cut out glow in the dark stars, his mind flashed back to a memory of him and Jessica lyin on the bed in the dark lookin all the stars on the ceilin, As Jessica pointed to one of the stars that were glowin bright she said, "Sunshine, you're goin to glow brighter than all of these stars when you become a famous."

"You think so, Satnin?" Austin asked, as he turned to look at her wonderin how come she had so much faith in him.

As she turned her head to look at him she said, "I don't think so. I know so because you make every person feel like you are singin to them."

"Are you sure every person feels that way?"

With a big laugh and sparkle in her eyes Jessica said, "Well, I know that you are singin to me whenever you sing a song."

Austin opened his eyes as tears ran down his face because he wished that Jessica was lyin right beside him in that moment. Austin started to wipe his eyes as he got up off the bed and made his way over the dresser. Just like any other time he was in her room Austin stepped on the one place in the wood floor that always creaked when you stepped on it. Jessica used to get so mad because she would always step on the spot, and her parents would always hear it if she was tryin to sneak out of her room. Austin soon stood in front of the dresser, and just stared at it for the longest time. His heart was beatin out of his chest as he thought about what would happen once he opened that drawer and found out the truth once and for all. Austin finally opened the third dresser drawer, reached clear to the back of it, and he pulled out a dark green sweater. Austin lost his breath for a minute because he remembered what the little girl said about how the black box was under the green sweater.

After catchin his breath, Austin put his hand back into the drawer and felt around until he found somethin. When he pulled his hand out there in his hand was the little black box, and Austin couldn't believe it. Austin looked down at the box for quite a while wonderin if he should open it or not. He wondered if he should go back home to his room and open it with no one around. After ponderin the question for about ten minutes Austin had made up his mind on what he was goin to do. Austin grabbed the green sweater, shut the dresser drawer, and walked out of the bedroom in a hurry. He saw that Mrs. Roth was in the kitchen gettin lunch started, so he darted out the door and down the driveway. He quickly made his way across the street and up his driveway to his front porch where he walked into the house.

Just as Austin walked into the house his father was settin in his easy chair watchin the PBS cookin television shows when he noticed Austin and he asked "Son, are you all right?"

"Yes, dad." Austin said, crackin a smile as he looked around the house. "I'm just goin to go upstairs to my room."

"What's that you got in your hand?"

"A sweater I found in the car. I forgot that I had left it in there so I'm goin to go put it up."

"All right." Austin's father said, concerned. "But you are sure that you are all right?"

"Yes, dad." Austin replied, as he started makin his way up the stairs to his bedroom.

After gettin into his room he locked the door and then sat on the bed just starin at the little black box. Deep down Austin really wasn't sure if his heart could take another surprise that let him know that Jessica was on the earth again. Austin knew he had just started to move forward with his life with Jaelyn, and he knew that keepin the knowledge that Jessica was alive again from Jaelyn would be wrong. Still, if it was true Jessica was alive again he wanted to keep it to himself. As all of the different scenarios run through his head about what might have been and what could be, Austin finally opened the little black box and found both the promise ring and the locket. As he held the promise ring in his hand tears fell from his eyes be-cause he knew that the man who took her away from him didn't get to pawn them or keep them. Austin was so overwhelmed that he started to cry because he had the truth in his hand that Jessica was alive on the earth again. Still, he wanted to know more about this thing called reincarnation. His head was still tellin him that it couldn't be real because of what he had learned in church, but his heart felt one hundred percent different about the subject.

That evenin around five o' clock the Reid family were just sittin down to supper when the phone started to ring, so Austin bein the last one in the kitchen leaned up against the wall as he picked the phone up and said, "Hello."

A familiar sweet southern voice asked, "Is Austin Reid there?"

"Speakin, who is this?"

"Austin, it's Eloise Killian." Eloise replied, with a smile and a big laugh.

"Hi, Eloise. How are you?"

"I'm doin good. Did you have a good time when you here down here in Mississippi?"

"Yes, I did."

"That's good. "

"How did you get my number?"

"I asked Larlee to get it for me from your cousin Lane."

"Ok. You wanted to talk to me that bad?"

"Yes, because you and I really didn't get to talk much over the two weeks you were here."

"Ok."   Austin said, a little confused by her explanation. "I thought you were datin David."

"We broke up, and he's goin out with Lee Ann now."

"That's interestin news."

"Do mind if I call you again sometime. The girls and I are thinkin about playin at Schlater's Diner next summer, and we would love for you to play with us for a few weeks."

"Sure, you can call me again some time."

Everyone at the dinin room table just looked at each other wonderin who Austin was talkin to because he seemed to know the person he was talkin to. His parents just wondered what Austin was doin talkin to another girl because that's all he needed to be doin.

"Ok." Eloise said, with a big smile. "I'll call you and let you know the details about playin this summer with us. Bye."

"All right." Austin said, before he hung up the telephone.

Austin picked up his plate from the kitchen island and made his way into the dinin room where everyone else was eatin. As Austin sat down in his chair his father looked over at him and asked, "Who was that girl you were talkin to?"

"She's just a girl I met in Mississippi over the summer." Austin explained, as he took a sip of his tea. "She and her friends have a band, and they want me to play with them next summer."

"Cool!" Brandon said, with a big smile as he looked across the table at his big brother.

"Are you goin to do it?" Rosanna asked, as she looked over at him as she took a bite of food.

"I'm thinkin about it." Austin replied. "I probably won't make up my mind until the spring."

"How long will you be gone?" Austin's mother asked, just wantin to know all the details.

"I don't know that. She said she was goin to call me back and let me know all the details."

"Ok, but you better start thinkin about where you are goin to go to college, Austin." Austin's father said, as he looked at his son very seriously.

Down here in Saltillo Eloise had hung up the phone and took a drink of her pop when Lee Ann broke the silence as she took a bite of popcorn and asked, "So, was he happy that you called, E?"

"Yes, I think so." Eloise said, as she looked over at Lee Ann.

"Are you goin to talk to him again?" Beverly asked, as she put a handful of popcorn in her mouth.

"Yes."

"Are you goin to chase after him?" Christine asked, crackin a big smile as she ate a handful of chocolate kisses.

"You know that I am."

"Is he why you broke up with David?" Lee Ann asked, wantin to get down to the truth so she could tell me.

"Maybe."

"You do know that he hung out with Rosanna Aydelotte most of the two weeks he was here." Beverly replied, as she stuck her hand back into the popcorn bag.

"I know he did." Eloise said, replied. "But what does that have to do with anything?"

"It might. What if he's datin her?" Lee Ann said, with a point.

"I hardly believe that because he's too young for her."

"In this society that doesn't mean anything."

"Most of our grandparents got married before the age of sixteen." Lee Ann said, havin a very good point.

"That's true." Eloise replied, realizin that Lee Ann did have a point. "Still, I think I have a chance with him."

As July turned into August many people in town were anticipatin the arrival of the Georgetown Fair, although for the kids in town it was a sign that summer was over and school would soon start. Many kids in town made that week of the Georgetown Fair really count as they got to stay up later and sleep in a little longer for the last week before school started the followin Monday.

On a hot muggy August night Austin was sleepin in his bed sound asleep, and in his dream he was swingin on Jessica's porch swing as the rain fell. He looked over and saw Jessica standin a few feet away just starin at him with the biggest smile on her face. Breakin the silence Jessica said, "You found my two most important things, didn't you?"

"Yes, Satnin, I did." Austin replied, crackin the biggest smile as he looked at her blue eyes.

As she walked over and sat down on the swing beside him Jessica said, "There is no doubt in your mind anymore because you have the proof right in front of you."

"There are some doubts because of what they taught us in church.." Austin said, with sadness in his eyes.

"You have to open your mind, and believe that somethin impossible can really happen"

"Really?"

"Yes, we have a second chance to be together."

"But, what if this is just some trick that's bein played on me."

"Austin Reid, I would never play a trick on you when it comes to us bein together again."

As he put his arm around her shoulder he said, "I know it will be worth the wait. It's just so hard to believe that you are back on the earth again."

"I am on the earth again." Jessica said, with a big smile on her face. "We have a chance to be together again, and have a relationship that will be unbreakable."

Just north of Georgetown on a country road Jaelyn was in her room sound asleep dreamin of Austin and her life together once everyone in town knew that they were datin. In her dream Jaelyn was so happy that Austin decided to stay in Illinois and not go to New York City to chase after his dreams. Austin's Grandpa Briggs wasn't doin very well, and Austin had do his work on the farm to keep it runnin. Austin was also goin to start his first semester at DACC, but he didn't know what he was goin to get his degree in. It was not surprisin that Reese and all her other close friends were tellin her that Austin would still leave town one day to chase after his dreams. The seeds of doubt were gettin deep into Jaelyn's mind as she watched Austin and wondered if he was really happy bein in his hometown. Then one night as the two set on Jaelyn's front porch swing the two were enjoyin the cool August breeze when

Jaelyn asked, "Austin, are you happy?"

"Of course, I'm happy." Austin replied, as he looked at her with a funny expression. "Why would you ask me a question like that?"

"Because you're still here in Georgetown, and not in the big city of New York." Jaelyn replied, as she ran her fingers over his right hand.

"Sweetness, I love bein here with you. Please don't doubt that."

"Cupcake, I know that you really wanted to go to New York."

Austin moved to where he was facin Jaelyn and said, "God has a different plan for me right now, but one day we will make it to New York together."

"You think so?" Jaelyn said, as she turned around to be face to face with him.

"Yes, I do."

Jaelyn cracked a smile as she put her hand in his and said, "Well, I am glad that you get to go with all my dances with me."

"That's all you're worried about." Austin said, crackin a grin as he laughed.

As Jaelyn gave Austin a kiss she said, "No, I love that we get to spend a lot time together."

"I love you, Sweetness." Austin said, crackin his boyish smile as he put his arms around her waist and pulled her closer to him.

Sound asleep in her bed Jaelyn smiled because she liked the dream she was havin with Austin stayin in town and goin to the local junior college. As she turned over and got comfortable in her bed, she hoped that it wouldn't be just a dream, but that Austin would stay in town after he graduated high school.

The Georgetown Fair started on Sunday afternoon, and everyone in town couldn't wait for Monday when the rides could be ridden. There were many proplr in town who went Sunday afternoon and evenin just to see what was goin on at the fairgrounds and to get somethin to eat. The next evenin the fair was packed with people as the rides started and it was the queen contest. Reese along with many of the girls in town were a little confused when

Austin showed up to the fair with Rosanna and not with Jaelyn. Although they were surprised that Jaelyn was happy to see Austin even though Rosanna was by his side that night.

Tuesday evenin was the talent contest and there were many contests in It. Austin and Jaelyn did their rehearsal performance in their allotted time. The other contests who were sittin the foldin chair seats watched them, and didn't really think much of the song that they were singin. After the rehearsal Austin and Jaelyn made their way out to the midway to get supper before the talent show started, as they set down at a table in the food buildin about ten feet away there was a young girl watchin them named Mallory Rossi. She was a tall bean pole of a girl with long dark brown hair and hazel eyes. She was goin to be an eighth grader at the junior high when school started the followin week. She was also good friends with Jaelyn, and she knew everything about Austin because Jaelyn would always talk about the time the two were spendin together.

As she watched Austin and Jaelyn bein playful with each other, Mallory was so jealous because she wanted it to be her. After eatin the two got up, threw their trash away, and held hands as they made their way down the midway lookin at all the games and rides that were there. Mallory walked down the midway behind them about five feet behind them, and she watched as Austin played a few games winnin prizes for Jaelyn. As Austin and Jaelyn started to make their way back to the track the two of them saw Mallory followin them, but neither one really thought much of it because she was their friend.. Austin did wonder if Jaelyn would be like Jessica and change her mind about goin on stage after their names were called. Two hours later the talent contest started right on time like it did every year. Austin and Jaelyn watched the younger children goin on stage to sing, and Austin was reminded when he was that young and performed on the stage for the first time. Finally, after what seemed like three hours Austin and Jaelyn's names were called, and as the two walked on the stage the crowd clapped for them.

After the two of them took a deep breath they started to sing

"The Lady Love's Me." from the Elvis Presley movie "Viva Las Vegas."

Many people in the crowd were very surprised that the two could sing so

well together. As Jaelyn sung the gentleman's all wet, she threw a bottle

of water at him. The crowd burst out in laughter because they thought it

was so funny and very unexpected. As the announcer walked back onto

the stage he asked, "Austin, are you all right?"

"Yes, sir." Austin said, as he took the towel from the announcer to dry

off his face.

"Did you know that she was goin to do that?"

"No, I didn't."

"Why do you think that she did that?"

"I don't know why my girlfriend would do that to me." Austin said,

crackin his boyish smile lookin at Jaelyn.

After he said that you could have heard a pin drop because everyone

was so quiet. People in the crowd were lookin at each other wonderin what was goin on, and why they hadn't heard that piece of information over the summer.

Breakin the silence the announcer asked, "Jaelyn, why would you throw water at your boyfriend?"

"Well, Elvis was pushed into a pool at the end of the song. "Jaelyn explained, with a big smile. "So, I figured throwin water on Austin would kind of help the crowd understand where we were goin the song."

"Ok, very good" The announcer said, crackin a big smile. "Our next contestant has competed since he was six years old, and claims that he's the best in Georgetown. Ladies and gentlemen, Robbie Wallison."

The crowd clapped as Austin and Jaelyn made their way off the stage, and Robbie took center stage. It was soon clear that Robbie had the crowd in the palm of his hand when he sang but would it be enough to win once again. When the talent show ended Austin and Jaelyn didn't win, but they had fun lettin the entire town know that they were boyfriend and girlfriend.

Fair week just like the years before seemed to fly by way too quickly, and before everyone knew it was Saturday. The demo derby was that night, and it always drew a big crowd every year. When Austin and his family got there the grandstands were halfway full, and it was good that Lane and her dad got there early enough to save everyone's seats. After gettin somethin to eat Austin and his family made their way up to the grandstands and found their seats. Not long after settin down Jaelyn and her family made their way up to the grandstands and set by Austin's family. Rosanna was talkin to them and the rest of the family havin a good time as she watched Austin and Jaelyn talkin. Rosanna was a little jealous of Jaelyn because Austin seemed to be in love with her while Rosanna was stuck in the friend's zone.

Durin a break between heats Austin made his way down to the bathroom because he had to go really bad, and he wanted to get another orange shake up to have somethin to drink. Austin stepped out of the bathroom and Reese pushed him up against the exhibit building givin him the most passionate kiss that she could. Austin was a little surprised and was caught off guard by Reese's actions. After the kiss was over Austin looked at her and asked, "Reesey, what was that about?"

"I'm so much better for you than Jaelyn." Reese said, crackin a little smile.

"I want to be with Jaelyn not you Reese." Austin said, with a very serious look.

"Does she know you're sleepin with Rosanna?"

"Where did you get that idea?"

"I see it by the way Rosanna looks at you, and if Jaelyn found out she'd leave you in a heartbeat."

"You're crazy."

"Do you want to dare me to tell Jaelyn, and see what she does?" Reese said, with a very serious look on her face.

"Reese, you need to move on because I'm not interested in you that way." Austin replied, with a very serious look on his face.

Reese just looked at him for a few minutes before she walked away from him not givin up hope that she could be with him one day. Austin made his way back up to the bleachers right before the next heat started. Rosanna watched Austin and Jaelyn as they wrapped their arms around each other to keep warm on that cold August night. Reese made her way back up to the bleachers and

61

set not too far from Austin, and she could see the jealousy in Rosanna's face as Rosanna watched Austin and Jaelyn.

The next Monday school started at Georgetown Ridge Farm high, school, and Austin couldn't wait to see what the school year held in store for him. Many weren't surprised when Austin and Jaelyn came into the high school holdin hands that first day. Lane, on the other hand, hated to go back because she was so ready to get away from the people that had bullied her for years. She was still recoverin from her surgery and still had a bad confession about herself every time she looked into the mirror. Lane also had to deal with her sister Harley bein a freshman that year, and what trouble she would get into because she liked to run her mouth without thinkin what she was sayin. Lane decided to keep her mind on her story Rodeo Dreams, and how she wrote how life could be for her in a world where she was popular and everything was goin right in her life.

On Sunday afternoon the Reid family gathered at Austin and Lane's grandma's house, and she had made chicken and noodles, mashed potatoes and gravy, corn, and a few desserts. while the grown-ups were in the dinin room talkin the kids were in the livin room watchin television.

On the television that evenin was Unsolved Mysteries and the
rerun a had segment on about two adult people rememberin their past
lives in a completely different era. Austin found it very interestin to watch.
Austin knew that Lane herself was wonderin if a past life she had was
affectin her life now because her life seemed to be obstacle after obstacle.
Many of the obstacles she seemed to have to get by again and again.
Austin decided to tell her because she would be the one who would understand what he had to tell her. Austin knew that his other family members
and friends would just think that he was crazy.

"Cous, what are you thinkin." Lane said, as she looked over at Austin
noticin that he was listenin very close to the program.

"Do you think Jessica would ever come back to earth?" Austin
replied, as he looked over at her wantin her opinion.

"Yes, I do. Her life was so short on the earth because it was taken
away from her by an evil man."

"Really?"

"Yes. Is there somethin you want to tell me? Spill it."

"Ok." Austin said, crackin his boyish smile. "When we went to Mississippi for those two weeks."

"Yes."

"Rosanna and I were in Schlatter's Diner and a little girl came in who was maybe two years old She stared at me for quite a while, and then said she was goin to marry me one day."

"Really?." Lane said, very interested in what he was tellin her.

"She told Rosanna that she was goin to steal me away from her. I asked her what her name was and she told me name was Jessica Lynn Roccha."

"You're kiddin me? No way!"

"No, I'm not." Austin said, still grinnin. "Anyway, the night of the catfish fry I went over and was talkin to the family, and Jessica told me where she had

put her necklace and the promise ring before she took her bike ride
that day."

"Yes, I remember that she always wore them. She always so proud
of those two pieces of jewelry."

"When they found her she wasn't wearin either one of them. So when
the little girl told me that I told her I would look for them. I was both scared
and hopeful at the same time."

"I can understand that, so when did you go to Jessica's house?"

"Last week after I took a walk I decided to see if I could find Jessica's
two most important things."

"You went for a walk? Ok."

"After I laid on the bed for a few minutes, I got the courage to look for
them."

"And what did you find?" Lane asked, on the edge of her seat.

"I found the green sweater she told me about." Austin said, crackin a little
grin as his eyes lit up. "I put my hand back in the drawer, and pulled out the
little black box that she said those two things were in."

"And what did you find?"

"I found the heart shaped locket I gave her, and the gold promise ring that she wore every day since the Christmas we exchanged them. "

"Oh, wow!" Lane said, a little shocked and amazed at the same time. "So she is your Jessica?"

"Yes, I think she is?"

"And what are you goin to do with that information?"

"Keep it to myself, and you can't tell a soul."

"Ok, cous." Lane replied, with a big smile. "Have you done any research on the subject?"

"No, I haven't.." Austin replied, with a big smile. "I was hopin that you would help me with that. I know that you have your own questions about livin a different life on earth before this one, and just like we learned about Elvis Presley we can learn about reincarnation."

"Sure, I'll help you, cous. Maybe we'll both find the answers we are lookin for."

"What are the two of you talkin about?" Rosanna asked, as she walked into the livin room and sat down on Austin's lap.

"Nothin important.." Lane replied, as she started to watch the television program that was on tv.

"What are you doin in here?" Austin asked, as he looked up into Rosanna's enchantin blue green eyes. "I thought you liked talkin to adults in my family."

"Their topic of conversation got too serious for me." Rosanna replied, as she looked into his ice blue eyes. "And the two of you seemed to be in a very serious conversation in here."

On August eighteenth Jesscia's kidnapper's second trial started, and Austin had told his parents that he was goin to be there every day to show that guy that Jessica did matter. Rosanna who had planned on leavin after the fair decided to stay, and go with Austin to the trial so that he would have support since both of his parents would be workin.

Jessica's parents were so happy that he was there with them along with other friends and family, but Mrs. Roth did hate that Austin had to hear the testimony about what happened to Jessica over again. She knew that it just about broke him the last time, but she was happy that Rosanna was there to be a shoulder to lean on when things in the courtroom got too tough for him. Jaelyn, on the other hand, felt so left out because she couldn't go to the trial, and Austin had stopped talkin to her when the trial started. She hated that he was turnin to Rosanna instead of her, and with Reese and the other girls were tellin her that Austin was probably sleepin with Rosanna because they were spendin all that time together. Jaelyn's mind went into overdrive as she thought about it every minute of every day.

On Sunday afternoon after eatin lunch Rosanna walked out onto the back deck to have a cigarette, Jaelyn, whose family had come over for lunch after church, followed her outside. As Rosanna lit her cigarette, Jaelyn sat down in a patio chair and asked, "Why are you tryin to steal Austin away from me?"

"I'm not tryin to steal him away from you." Rosanna replied, as she turned around to look at her. "I'm just here as his friend."

"Well, since you're here and goin to the trial with him he isn't talkin to me very much."

"Jaelyn, that's not because of me."

"You forget that I heard you say that if he didn't have a girlfriend you would like to be." Jaelyn said, remindin her of that summer day.

"I know that I said that." Rosanna replied, as she flipped ashes from her cigarette off into the ash tray as she sat down in a patio chair across from Jaelyn.. "But he loves you Jaelyn, and he wants to be with you.."

"You think he's in love with me?"

"I know that he is."

"How can you be sure?"

"I see the way he looks at you when you around him. Have you ever noticed the way he looks at you?"

"Really? No, I haven't."

"You are very special to him, and he loves you so much, It's just the trial is weighin on his mind because of all the memories it has brought up."

"I know." Jaelyn said, with a big smile knowin that Rosanna was right.

"He was so upset when he learned that guy got a new trial."

"Just give him some time he's dealin with a lot right now." Rosanna said, very seriously. "He's havin to hear all the bad stuff that guy did to her all over again, and he's not handlin it well."

"I didn't know that..."

"You just need to give him some time, and let him work through it

"Here I am bein selfish because I'm so afraid that he's turnin to you because I won't give him certain things." Jaelyn replied, as she looked at Rosanna with fear in her eyes.

"Just turn your focus onto takin care of Austin, and everything will work out just fine." Rosanna said, with a big smile knowin that Jaelyn was right about the two of them bein together it was just before the trial that it started.

About an hour later Austin went to the back door to check on Rosanna and Jaelyn, and he was surprised to find them laughin and havin a good time. He started to wonder what they had bonded over because in the middle of July the two didn't like each other at all. He hoped that the two had found common ground to stand on, and that they would be good friends.

On Thursday afternoon after the jury was given the case on Monday afternoon, they had finally come back with a verdict. Jessica's mother didn't know what the verdict would be because it was a different jury. She took a sigh of relief when the jury's verdict came back guilty on all counts once again. The courtroom irrupted in cheers because that man would be behind bars, and could not hurt anyone else. Rosanna was so happy to see a smile on Austin's face because it was finally over for him. He wouldn't have to sit in a courtroom again and hear all the things that the evil man did to Jessica.

On Saturday mornin Austin and Jaelyn took Rosanna to catch her flight in Indianapolis to go home to NYC, and both were sad to say goodbye to her.

She told them that she would be talkin to them soon enough because she had both of their phone numbers and planned on checkin in on two of them. both the ride home Austin and Jaelyn talked about everything that was botherin them at the time. Jaelyn felt good that Austin wasn't hidin anything from her, and the two didn't have any secrets between them.

The weeks seemed to pass quickly with both football season and volleyball season goin strong at GRHS, Austin was at every home and away volleyball game cheerin on Jaelyn and Jaedyn. Many nights he brought his homework with him to do because with football practice he didn't have time to work on it before goin to the games. And it was no surprise that Jaelyn was at every football game that Austin had both home and away. Many people thought that might change as the September chill came into the air, and the date got closer to the twentieth. Austin and the Roth family also got news that Jessica's killer filed for appeal in his case, and the wondered if he would get another trial.

On Monday September fourteenth homecomin week started at GRHS, and many of the students couldn't wait to get the week started. There would be a theme to dress up every day, and on Friday there was the annual homecomin games.

Many of the freshmen thought it was pretty cool, and most of the other classes were used to it by now. Many students that day were askin other students to go to the homecomin dance on Saturday night, so that they would already have their couldn't wait to start workin on the floats for the parade on Wednesday night, so they could feel special as they walked down the main street of Georgetown.

On Friday afternoon all the teenagers from the different grades set on the bleachers on the home side of the football field, and the preteen from Mary Miller Junior High set on the away bleachers on the other side of the field. It was no surprise that many of the participants in the games were the popular teenagers in the different classes, but on occasion there were teen-agers who weren't popular that did participate. That year Austin participated in a few of the games, and Jaelyn also participated in the games. Lane set on the bleachers watchin really wantin to have a pencil and paper in hand so she could write. Harley also participated in the homecomin games, and she thought it was really fun. That night the homecomin football game was a nail bitter because it was a tough game for the Buffaloes, but Austin made some good plays surprisin many people. At half-time the homecomin queen was announced, and many weren't surprised when Elieen's name was called because she was very popular in her own class along with the other three classes that were in the high school.

On Saturday afternoon Lane was readin the latest things about past lives that she had printed out at her mom's house. The last couple of years she had started to wonder if she had been on the earth before because every-one kept tellin her that she seemed to be wiser than her years. Lane hadn't really thought about it that much, but readin the information she had found online she did start to wonder. She also thought that maybe it would also explain her crush on the teacher Mr. Somerled that she had since she was a freshman in high school. Mr. Somerled was a tall muscular man with dark brown hair, and eyes that told his feelins. She remembered the first time they looked at each other when she was in his history class, and how intense the moment was when their eyes met. She also began to remember when it went around the school that he had cheated on his wife with another teacher, and how his oldest daughter started a scuffle with the other teacher besides callin her every name in the book. The cops were called to break up the fight because his daughter got some good punches in givin the teacher two black eyes. She knew that in the church they believed that you only live one life, and if you had accepted Jesus you go up to heaven to be with God. Part of her questioned that belief because Mr. Somerled seemed to feel like a familiar soul to her, but she just didn't know where the puzzle pieces fit in.

It was also the night of the homecomin dance, but Lane wasn't goin to go because she felt like it would only give those teenagers who made fun of her another reason to laugh at her. In Lane's mind she could work on her great novel that was goin to change the world one day, and she didn't have any time for the teenager's stuff. No surprise that Harley had a date and was goin to it, an Austin was taken Jaelyn to the dance.

Around nine o' clock at the dance the song "The Moon Over Georgia" started to play, and Jaelyn wanted Austin to dance with her, but he told her no and found a seat on the bleachers watchin everyone dancin in the middle of the gym floor. Austin closed his eyes and in his mind he saw Jessica standin in front of him. She was dressed in a long green dress with her amber brown hair on her shoulders lookin at him. Jessica had a twinkle in her blue green eyes and a smile on her face when she said, "Sunshine, are you goin to set every dance out or are you goin to dance with me?"

"Sorry, Satnin." Austin replied, crackin his boyish grin as he looked up at her. "I was just lookin at how beautiful you are."

"Thank you." Jessica said, with a smile as she took his hand and led him to the dance floor. "I love this song."

"You know that's all I have to offer you right now is the moon."

"And I would choose you over any other man who could offer me everything."

"You would?" Austin asked, as he lookin into her lovin blue green eyes.

About ten feet away Jaelyn, Jaedyn, Reese, Peyton, Elieen, Hope, Maddie, and a few others were watchin Austin as he sat on the bleachers. They all wondered who he was thinkin about as he sat there with his eyes closed. Reese had started datin Kerim Padilla at the beginnin of the year to make Austin think that she had moved on from him. Reese couldn't stand it any longer she broke the silence by sayin, "Who do you think Austin is thinkin about?"

"Jessica." Peyton said, as she watched Austin's expression. "Because she was the only one who could get him to smile that way."

"You're probably right." Jaelyn replied, with sadness in her voice.

"You all right, sis?" Jaedyn said, as she looked at her sister concerned.

"Didn't he sing this song at the talent show one summer?"

"Yes, the summer of nineteen ninety-one." Hope answered, enterin the conversation.

"And you know who he was singin the song to when he was on stage."

"Yes, I know who sang that song too." Jaelyn replied, as she looked over at Peyton.

"Are you goin to be able to deal with the ghost of Jessica in your relationship for the rest of your life?" Peyton asked, as she looked at Jaelyn.

"I'm goin to have to… It's the only way I can be with Austin."

"You are braver than I would ever be." Eileen said, puttin her two cents into the conversation.

"I don't think I could live knowin that there will always be a third person in my relationship." Reese said, hittin on of Jaelyn's button to make her worry.

"I'm beginnin to wonder that myself." Jaelyn said, with a worried look on her face. "Just knowin that he will always compare me to her for the rest of my life."

On Sunday mornin Austin came with his family to church, and not long after gettin there he walked over to talk to Jaelyn. As Austin's mother watched Austin with Jaelyn, she could see that Jaelyn was an angel sent from God to help her son start to live his life again. She didn't want to think about what might have happened if Jaelyn hadn't have come into his life when she did. Austin's mother hated to think that her son might not be alive because he went into such a dark place that he killed himself because of the grief over losin Jessica. Church started a few minutes late that mornin because everyone was talkin about what happened at homecomin the night before. Austin started to sit down in his seat when he saw Jaelyn smile at him, so he smiled back at her. After the mornin hymns were sung the preacher walked up to the podium and as he turned page in his bible he said, "Please turn to Matthew 3:1 in your bible and when you get there say amen."

Within a few moments many people in the congregation said amen, and the preacher looked up at them and said, "John the Baptist is preachin in the wilderness of Judea sayin repent your old way of thinkin. Regret past sins and live your life in a way that proves repentance. Seek God's purpose for your life for the kingdom of heaven is at hand. He reminded them this was the one mentioned by the prophet Isaiah. Isaiah said that the voice shoutin in the wilderness prepares the road for the lord makes his highways straight. John had clothin made of camels' hair and a leather band. His food was locusts and wild honey."

"Oh, come on." The elderly men in the back row said, with a big smile.

"In Luke 15:10 Jesus is teachin a parable. A woman has lost a coin in her house that is equal to a day's wages. When she finds it she calls friends and neighbors to say rejoice with me because I have found the lost coin. Jesus also says that the angels are filled with joy when one sinner repent of their sin and seeks the lord for their purpose."

"Preach it!"

"If you are in sin right now and think that it is fun. You are hurtin yourself because you will never live the purpose for your life because you are enjoyin the fire of the devil as you turned away from the lord. You will go into the lake of fire, and will not be in the presence of the lord because he will say that he doesn't know you."

"Oh, yea." An elderly woman said, with a big smile. "Tell them all about it, preacher."

"Repent of sin!" The preacher yelled, as he wiped his forehead with a handkerchief.

"Once you repent of your sins your heart will be clean, and you can have a fresh start with the lord. John the Baptist baptized with water, but now that Jesus is the one baptizin, and you'll be baptized with fire changin your life forever."

"Amen!" A few people in the congregation yelled in agreement with him.

After the preacher said the endin prayer, the quietness was broken with chatter as many people caught up with the local gossip of the week. Austin made his way up to the stage where Jaelyn was talkin to some of her friends as she made her way out of the choir box. Jaelyn kissed Austin as he got close to her which surprised many of the people in the congregation because they didn't feel anyone should do that in the sanctuary. Austin and Jaelyn did notice that Mallory was sittin in one of the pews just watchin them, and it did make them wonder why she would be starin at them.

Three weeks later on a chilly Wednesday October late afternoon in New York City on the set of Americana at Rodman Studios Rosanna was sittin in her dressin room takin her lunch break when the dressin room door opened and Kelli King stepped in and asked, "So how are things goin with Austin these days?"

"Things are good." Rosanna said, as she looked over at her as she looked up from the most recent picture. "He and I write letters to each other still, and we talk on the telephone occasionally."

Just as she answered Kelli's question castmates Brittany Rhea, Christina Fuller, a short skinny dark-haired beauty with dark eyes, and Margret, Coppel, a tall average skinny blonde woman with light blue eyes and a bubbly attitude, walked in the room and Christina asked, "Who is this Austin person?"

"He's the boy I went to have Thansgivin with in nineteen ninety-six."

"You have a boyfriend?" Margret asked, a little surprised as she looked around the room. "When did this happen? Where was I?"

"No, he's not my boyfriend. He's just a very good friend."

"Why isn't he your boyfriend? Since the two of you seem to talk all the time." Christina asked, as she looked at her with a funny expression.

"He has a girlfriend in his hometown, and she's very nice."

"Wait, you met his girlfriend?" Christina said, as she sat down in the easy chair.

"Yes, when I went home with him over the summer, and he showed me around town."   Rosanna replied, as she looked over at Christina.

"He is a good kisser." Brittany said, with a big smile as she leaned up against the door.

"How would you know?" Margret asked, as she looked over at Brittany.

"I kissed him over the summer when Rosanna and I went down to visit Kelli in Mississippi."

"Yes, I know you did." Rosanna replied. "Austin told me all about it."

"He did?" Brittany said, still wearin a big smile.

"Who is this girlfriend of his?"

"She is a freshman in high school."

"You let a freshman in high school take the man that you wanted?"

"Well, he asked her to date him after the Thanksgivin holiday in nineteen ninety-six."

"Are you goin to go after him?" Margret asked, with a big grin as she looked around at all the other girls.

"No, I'm not goin to go after him."

"I would go after him." Brittany asked, crackin a big smile.

"Of course, you would."

"I would too…" Marget said, smilin.

"Oh boy..." Rosanna said, laughin.

"What does he look like?" Marget asked, really wantin to see a picture of him.

"Here's the last picture we took together before I left Illinois." Rosanna said, as she took the picture frame from her desk and handed it to Margret.

Margret smiled as she looked at the picture before handin it to Christina, with a big smile she said, "Austin is very cute, and he's goin to be a heartbreaker."

"He already is, and when he becomes famous he'll break even more hearts." Rosanna said, as she set the picture back on the makeup table.

Down here in Saltillo, Mississippi, I was part of the popular group of kids, but, I also had a lot of friends who weren't popular that other kids made fun of. I stood up for them when I could, but even I was cautious because I didn't want to lose havin popular status with everyone. Eloise, Lee Ann, Beverly, and Christine were, of course, part of the popular crowd. Everyone in town knew who they were along with their families havin money.

I really wasn't payin attention in my classes because I found school so borin. I would compare it to a Sunday sermon at church sometimes because I was just not wantin to takin in the information that I was supposed to be gettin.

The holiday season seemed to creep up on all of us. Thanksgivin came way too fast, and within three weeks we were all on Christmas break. After celebratin Christmas everyone in the world was gettin ready to leave the year we were in and welcome the new year comin. Just like any other year people were filled with excitement and wonder as they thought about what the new year would bring them. That January there was an ice storm that hit Canda and the Northwestern United States causin destruction, Nineteen European nations agree to forbid human clonin, A women's clinic in Alabama is bombed with one person killed. That year the first two months of nineteen ninety-eight were the hottest on record and there was only 4.6 inches of snow when a a normal winter the state of would have gotten 16 inches. The lowest tempe-rature was six degrees.

The new year started good for Lane because she had learned so much about reincarnation and past lives. She learned that in every new life that we live we either are learnin the lessons we didn't learn in our past lives or we are learnin new lessons. Just like Austin, Lane did find it hard to comprehend because it wasn't jivin with what the preachers were sayin. Lane couldn't understand how we could live in our spirit for eternity since when she had read that comin to earth is the greatest test our spirit will have.

On a very cold January evenin Lane had gone to bed thinkin about what she had read that day, and how some of us are young souls while others are old souls. She did wonder what kind of soul she was because she knew she didn't have very much life experience in the life she was livin because she chose to hide from the world. Lane was so afraid of what other people thought and were sayin about her. Two hours later she finally went off to dreamland and was sleepin very soundly.

In her dream she was openin up a classroom door and walkin into it, and settin at the desk was a tall muscular man with dark brown hair and blue eyes that talk to you without sayin a word. As Lane walked over to the desk with a big smile on her face she said, "Do you have time for me, Mr. Ainsley?"

"I always have time for you." Mr. Ainsley said, crackin a big smile as he looked up at her from his papers.

As Lane got past the desk, she walked over and set in Mr. Ainsley lap. The two passionately kissed each other makin most of the time they had by themselves. After the kiss was over Lane ran her fingers through his hair and said, "I know that we don't have much time because we don't want anyone to catch us, but I had to give you one kiss before I left school for the day."

"Raine, you know better than to kiss me while were here at school. Why are you bein so careless?"

"Because I love kissin you. Plus, I know at my parents' party tonight you will bring your wife and daughters to the party, and I won't get to spend any time alone with you."

"Raine, you know that we'll sneak a moment or two together alone." Mr. Ainsley said, crackin a big grin.

"I don't know." Raine said, with a little grin. "Your wife watches you like a hawk."

"That's true, but she can't keep her eyes on me all night long when she will be talkin to other people at the party."

"I know, but what if we get caught?"

"We might get caught." Mr. Ainsley said, as he kissed her on the lips.

"But I love spendin every moment with my sweet baby."

"I think I'm fallin for you, Mr. Ainsley." Raine said, crackin a smile, as she got up off his lap and made her way to the classroom door.

Raine unlocked and walked out of Mr. Ainsley classroom just as the principal started to walk down the hallway toward the rooms. She met the principal about halfway down the hall, and he asked her what she was doin in Mr. Ainsley classroom after school had let out for the day. Raine explained that she had a few questions about the assignment he had given, and wanted to be clear about what her paper had to write. The principal seemed to be satisfied with her answer, and continued to walk down the hallway doin his after school ritual. He didn't even go into Mr. Ainsley room to check Raine's story.

Lane woke up in a cold sweat as she set straight up in her bed. She couldn't' believe what she had dreamed and who she had dreamed of. As she thought about what she had dreamed, Lane could see herself doin that if she was more confident to go after what she wanted, but she was so unsure of herself that she knew she wouldn't be able to do it at that point in time. Lane did start to think that maybe her and Mr. Somerled were together in another life because in her dream the two seemed very in love with each other. Lane laid back down and tried to go to sleep, but her mind kept driftin off to feelin Mr. Somerled lips and how passionately he kissed her.

January turned into February and soon it was time for the Valentine's Day dance at the high school on Saturday night. Austin really didn't want to go to another dance, but Jaelyn wanted to go so he told her he would go. The afternoon before the dance Austin had laid down on his bed to take a nap because he knew that he would be exhausted by the time the dance was over. He had just fallen asleep, and he was soon in dreamland. In his dream Austin and Jessica were lyin on a king size bed snugglin with each other. As he ran his hand up and down her arm Austin said, "Can you believe that we are finally in NYC together?"

"No, I can't believe it." Jessica replied, as she listened to his heartbeat.

"Or that we are goin to be models for the same clothin company."

"No, I can't believe that either." Jessica said, as she lifted her head to look into his ice blue eyes.

Jaelyn's sister had dropped her off at Austin's house so that they could go to the dance together. Plus, Jaelyn wanted to have some alone time with him before the dance since it was Valentine's Day. She had said hello to every-one on his family before she made her way upstairs to Austin's room where she found him sleepin on his bed. She walked into the room, and sat on his brother Brandon's bed just watchin him sleep. Austin had a smile on his face, and Jaelyn hoped that she was the one puttin that smile on his face.

Back in Austin's dream he and Jessica were still just starin into each other's eyes and havin their conversation. Still lookin into his eyes Jessica said, "Sunshine, we are finally gettin to live out the dreams we dreamed while I was alive in my old life."

"Back then you were nowhere near the stage or the camera."

"I know, but in this life I'm goin to be right beside you when it comes to the two of them."

"I know." Austin said, crackin his boyish grin. "What changed what changed your mind?"

"I saw why you loved bein in front of a crowd so much, and I wanted to be part of it with you." Jessica said, as she gave him a kiss.

"I love that you want to be part of it with me, and that you understand why I love it so much."

"The fact that the owner of the clothin company thinks we'll look good together as his models is just a plus."

"And so is the movie that we're goin to be starrin in together."

"Hopefully, the first of many."

"Yes…" Austin said, as he moved a piece of hair out from in front of her eye.

"Since we're talkin seriously I don't want to share you anymore with Jaelyn."

"Really?"

"I've waited most of my life to be with you, and now that I'm old enough to be with you I don't want to share you with anyone." Jessica said, as she gave him a kiss.

In a split-second Austin's dream changed, and now he was standin at the kitchen sink lookin out the window when Jaelyn walked into the room with a magazine in her hand.. As she held up the magazine Jaelyn asked,, "Who is she?"

"Jaelyn, what are you talkin about?" Austin asked, as he turned around to look at her as he dried his hands with a dish towel.

"Who is this woman in the picture with you?"

"Her name is Jessica Roccha, and she's a member of the Schlatter's."

"Why is she in the picture with you?" Jaelyn asked, raisin her voice.

"The president of the Ruzzio clothin company saw us singin together, and asked her to be a model of the new line of women's clothes comin out in May."

"Are you sleepin with her?"

"No, why?"

"Well, Austin. I have a hard time believin that you're tellin me the truth. After learnin that you lied to be about really bein Lucas' father, and all the rumors about you bein with other women from your television show."

"Sweetness, Jessica and I are just friends." Austin said, seein the hurt in her eyes. "It's not a big deal."

"The hell it isn't." Jaelyn said, as she threw the magazine at him as she stomped out of the kitchen headin down the hallway.

Austin woke up quickly as he saw what happened last in his dream, and as he looked toward the closet he saw Jaelyn settin in Brandon's bed lookin at him. As he set up against the headboard Austin cracked his boyish grin and said, "How long have you been settin there?"

"Long enough to see that your dream was intense by the look on your face." Jaelyn replied, walkin over to the bed over sittin down on the bed beside him. "What were you dreamin about?"

"You and I in the future as husband and wife."

"Really?"

"Yes, really."

"I do hope that happens in the future." Jaelyn said, as she leaned back against him and put her hand in his.

"What?" Austin replied, as he kissed her on the cheek.

"Me becomin Mrs. Austin Reid."

"Do you think you can handle bein Mrs. Austin Reid?"

"I believe I can handle it." Jaelyn said, with a big smile. "I get you better than anyone else in this world."

"Really?" Austin said, as he started kissin her on the neck. "Can we stay here tonight? I really would like to spend Valentine's Day with only you and not with our friends."

"Yes." Jaelyn said, with a big smile and a giggle. "And I love that we'll have our own little dance."

That night Austin and Jaelyn listened to Elvis's music along with other music, and danced to a few songs. They also just hung out on the bed together and talked about their lives in the future. Jaelyn wasn't too happy that in Austin's future of them he had become a star, and she was right beside him on the red carpet as the many lights from cameras went off takin their picture. In tellin her future for them they still lived in this little town Austin worked for his grandpa, and she was a nurse, and the two had a house full of kids. They also lived in Jaelyn's grandparent's house that was a hundred yards away from her parents' house.

Winter turned into spring, but it seemed like it took forever for it to happen. Austin didn't even run track that year because he spent all of his free time with Jaelyn. By this time Jaelyn's parents had noticed how in love Austin and Jaelyn were, and they were happy for the two of them. As March turned into April many of people of the senior and junior class were gettin ready to go the last dance of their school career, and Lane really wasn't very excited about goin to it. Still, she knew it would be the last dance in her high school career, so she decided to go with a group of people but felt like a fish out of water. That night people weren't surprised that Austin and Jaelyn came to the dance together. They had a lot of fun just dancin to the music that was bein played by the DJ. Jaelyn wasn't jealous at all when Austin danced with Reese, Hope, and a few other girls from the two classes. It also wasn't long before Harley showed up with her date Rusty Smuth and started dancin with Austin and Jaelyn. While Austin and Harley were havin fun Austin saw Lane sittin in a chair just watchin everyone else and not lookin like she was enjoyin herself at all.

The next mornin the seniors went on their senior trip to Florida, and Lane had decided to go. Lane was nervous the entire trip because she didn't trust her classmates because many of them had teased and been mean to her throughout the years in school. While her roommates at the hotel went out on the town, she was in the hotel room writin on her novel Rodeo Dreams and listenin to music. She liked the time she got to be by herself because it was a chance for her nerves to calm down, and she could finally relax from all the anxiety she was feelin. While at Disneyland while many of her classmates were off ridin rides and doin their own thing, she and a few of her classmates ended up hangin around a few teachers as they walked around the park. Mr. Somerled was one of those teachers in the group, and Lane liked that she got to be both close and talk to him.

Four weeks later on May 23, 1998, Lane graduated from Georgetown Ridge Farm High School. As she walked out of the high school she yelled at her mom that she made it because there were a few years her parents didn't know if she was goin to make it or not since her grades were so poor.

All three of her grandparents were so proud of her for graduatin high school because they themselves didn't graduate from high school because of circumstances of their time. Grandma Sutton liked it because she could brag on her to the family down south about what she had accomplished just like she had done with her own children.

Chapter Two

A Look At The Past

As May turned into June Austin and Jaelyn were happy spendin as much time together as they could that summer. Austin had told Jaelyn that he was goin to go to Mississippi when he heard from a member of the band that he was playin with.. Jaelyn didn't like it because she had wanted to have Austin all to herself that summer because the next school year was his senior year. She was still so afraid that he would leave town while she was still in high school, and she would lose him forever. She talked both her parents and his parents into lettin her stay with Austin the week of his birthday, and Austin's parents promised that they would keep an eagle eye on the two of them since Jaelyn was only fifteen, and Austin was turnin eighteen on Saturday. Austin and Jaelyn spent a lot of time in the pool and watched his younger brother and sister as the summer.

As a warm breeze blew on a Thursday evernin Austin and Jaelyn laid on the guest bedroom bed just starin at each other and makin conversation. As she looked down at the bed wantin and not wantin to know the answer Jaelyn looked up and asked, "Did you ever have sex with Rosanna?"

"Sweetness, why do you want to know that?" Austin asked, as he cracked his boyish grin shocked she would ask that question.

"I just want to know if you did?"

"And what if I tell you that I did. Are you goin to be upset?"

"I might be a little bit.." Jaelyn replied, lookin into his ice blue eyes.

"Ok, the truth is…"

"The truth is what?"

"I have had sex with Rosanna, and it happened when she was here celebratin Thanksgivin in nineteen ninety-six."

"Did you sleep with her over the summer in nineteen ninety-seven when she came home with you from Mississippi?"

"No, sweetness, I didn't."

"Why haven't you had sex with me?" Jaelyn asked, as she started runnin her fingers through his hair.

"You're not ready for that." Austin replied, with a very serious look on his face.

"Why?"

"Because you only want to do it because you're afraid I'll turn to someone else if you don't."

"I do feel that way." Jaelyn explained, with a serious look on her face. "Because you are goin to be five hundred miles away, and I'm sure girls will be chasin after you."

"Nothin is goin to happen because I love you."

"Cupcake, I'm just scared that I'm goin to lose you.."

"You are not goin to lose me."

"I'm just really scared that I will one of these days." Jaelyn said, as tears fell from eyes.

Austin cracked his boyish grin and softly kissed Jaelyn on the lips, and Jaelyn kissed Austin back so passionately. Austin pulled her closer to him as the moment got very intense for the two of them as he got on top of Jaelyn, he started to unbutton Jaelyn's shirt, and he waited for her to say stop. To Austin's surprise the two were very close to havin sex with each other before she said stop, and the two spent the night wrapped up in each other's arms. Jaelyn lay in bed next to Austin as he slept soundly, and she looked up at the cecilin thinkin that she should have gone all the way with him.

A few days later it was Austin's seventeenth birthday, and his family had a big pool party for him. Austin's mother could see there was tension between him and Jaelyn, and she knew that it was probably because he was leavin sometime that summer to go to Mississippi. The group of people that were at Austin's party all seemed to be havin a good time. Austin's mother did notice that Austin's best friend Remy Gagliardo was talkin to Jaelyn and lettin her know that if she ever wanted to hang out he'd like to. She saw that Austin hadn't noticed that his best friend was makin a move on his girlfriend because he was talkin to all the other guests at the party.

Late that afternoon the telephone rang at the Reid house, and Austin's mother answered it. A woman asked if Austin was there, and his mother told her to hold on a minute while she went and got him. She yelled at Austin through the back screen door and told him he had a phone call. Austin made his way out of the pool and into the house. As he picked up the phone from the ledge next to the phone he said, "Hello."

"Austin, hello." A sweet southern voice said, excited to hear his voice.

"Eloise, how are you doin? "Austin replied, as he cracked a big grin happy to finally hear from her.

Jaelyn walked into the house just as he said that because she wanted to know who he was talkin to. She made her way to the kitchen island to get somethin from the vegetable tray. As she dipped her carrot into the ranch dip and put it in her mouth, she looked over at Austin and smiled at him.

"I'm good, I wanted to tell you that we are playin at Schlatter's diner the last two weeks of June."

"Ok.."

"You need to come down the weekend before because we are spendin a few days in New York City." Eloise explained, as she looked at the other girls. "We are goin to see the Broadway musical Smokey Joe's Café."

"Ok." Austin said, a little surprised that they would want him to go with them.

"We want you to be in our band, and when we get famous we want to have our own show at the local theater just like it in the same way."

"Oh cool, that's a great idea."

"So, we'll will see you on June twelfth or thirteenth."

"Yes, you will."

"Ok." Eloise said, crackin a little smile happy that Austin was comin down the next weekend.

"See you next weekend." Austin said, crackin his boyish grin before he hung up the telephone.

After she saw Austin hang up the phone, Jaelyn leaned up against the kitchen island she said, "So you are leavin next weekend?"

"Yes,."

"I guess I better make the most of this next week before you leave for Mississippi."

Austin walked over and put his arms around her waist and said,
"Yes, you better.."

Jaelyn giggled as she put her arms around his neck and gave him a kiss. Outside lookin into the house Remy was watchin the two of them, and wonderin if he would ever have a chance with Jaelyn. He could very clearly that the two were in love with each other, but Remy was fallin hard for Jaelyn with each new day. Remy just hoped that Austin would mess up and lose Jaelyn so that he could be with her.

The next week seemed to go by quickly but slowly at the same time, and it was Friday mornin already. Austin drove over to Jaelyn's house to visit her before he left for Mississippi for three weeks.. When he pulled up in the

108

driveway he took a deep breath, walked to the front door, and knocked
on it, Mrs. Somerled answered the door and said, "Hi, Austin, come on in."

"Is Jaelyn here?" Austin asked, as he walked into the house and saw her
dad sittin on the couch watchin television.

"Yes, she is in her room, I think."

Austin just smiled as he started walkin up the stairs to the second floor.
When he got to the doorway of her room Austin saw Jaelyn sound asleep
with her arms around a pillow. Crackin his boyish grin he walked into the
room, sat down on the bed, leaned over and gave Jaelyn a kiss on the
cheek. As Jaelyn opened her eyes Austin said, "Hi, sweetness. How are
you?"

"I'm all right." Jaelyn replied, as she looked into Austin's lovin blue eyes.

"You and I are goin to spend the entire day together since I leave for
Mississippi tomorrow."

"Do you really have to go?"

"Yes, I told them that I would play in their band with them this summer."

109

"I don't want to you to leave me."

"The next three weeks will go by so fast you won't have time to miss me."

"You know that I'll miss you."

Just then Jaedyn walked into the doorway of Jaelyn's room and said, "You better not hurt my sister while you're gone this summer."

"You're not helpin me, Jade." Austin said, as he looked over at her.

"I'm just givin you a warnin that you better be true to my sister the three weeks that you are away from G'town."

"I know, and if I'm not you're goin to beat me up."

"Damn right!" Jaedyn said, crackin a big smile as she winked at him.

Jaelyn looked up at Austin and grinned from ear-to-ear knowin that if he did do anything to break her heart Jaedyn would beat him up. Austin just shook his head as he saw how Jaelyn and Jadyn ganged up on him. He knew that he didn't stand a chance of winnin the conversation with the two of them.

"Just remember." Jaedyn said, as she started to walk down the hallway. "You hurt my baby sister I will hurt you, Austin Reid."

"I got it, Jade." Austin said, with his boyish grin lettin her know that she had made her point.

Austin and Jaelyn spent time at her house before they decided to go out for pizza and to the mall. That evenin they went to his house and swam in the pool, and just talked about the future they were goin to have together once the two of them got out of high school. Austin went first and told her that he was goin to be a famous star and she would be his wife and walk the red carpet with him. Jaelyn's vision Austin stayed in Georgetown to be with her, and the two got married and had a family together. They settled down and lived in her grandparents' house not far from her parent's house.

Early the next mornin Austin put his suitcases in the trunk of his ford mustang. He then put the electric guitar in the back seat along with his amp, and put the driver's side seat back before he got into the car. Austin made his way down the end of the driveway, and looked over at Jessica's house as he pushed an Elvis Presley cd into the cd player. The song "Lovin You" was the first song that started to play, and memories of singin that song to Jessica came floodin back as tears filled his eyes. Austin pulled out of the driveway and made his way through town to the stop light. Once the light turned green Austin turned south and started his journey to Mississippi. After a long eight-hour car ride Austin stopped at a gas station on the south side of Memphis and called Eloise to tell her he was an hour away. Eloise was excited because he was so close, and she told him that she and the girls would be waitin on him when he got there.

When he pulled into the Schlatter Farm driveway he couldn't believe how long the driveway was. He saw Eloise, Lee Ann, Beverly, and Christine were there waitin on him outside of a little house. After he parked the car and stepped out of it Beverly said, "Hey, Yankee what are you doin down this way?"

"I came to visit with some friends that I made last summer." Austin said, crackin a big smile as he shut the car door.

"Why are you wearin a pair of Elvis sunglasses." Eloise said, as she walked over and gave him a hug.

112

"I love my sunglasses." Austin said, with a big smile as he hugged her "I'm goin to be a star someday and I'll need them."

"Did you bring your guitar?" Christine asked, she enjoyed the sun shinin on her face.

"Yes, I did."

"Good." Beverly said, crackin a little grin as she looked over at him. "Did you bring a song list or sheet music for us to learn the songs you want to sing?"

"Yes, I did.." Austin said, as he leaned up against his car.

"We are goin to have so much fun this summer." Eloise said, still Still havin her arms around Austin's neck.

Austin and the girls caught up for the next hour about what had happened in their lives since the last time they had seen each other. gave Austin the keys to the guesthouse which was right next to Eloise. the girls then went to their own houses as they watched Austin get his stuff out of the car.

Austin got settled into his guest house and soon took a nap because the nine-and-a-half-hour trip had kicked his butt. He had just gotten to sleep when and in his dream he was in a guest house like he was in. As he laid in bed someone walked into the doorway and said, "Benny, we have to tell my sister about us."

"Amelia, you know that we can't do that." Benjamin replied, as he looked over at her.

As Ameila walked over to the bed and sat down on the bed beside Benjamin she said, "I know that the two of you broke up, but she thinks that you are goin to work out your problems and get back together."

"Lia, come on you know that she and I aren't goin to get back together."

"Well, you need to tell her that."

"That doesn't matter." Benjamin said, as he leaned up and kissed her on cheek. "Because I want to be with you."

Benjamin just cracked a little grin as he leaned up and gave Amelia a soft but passionate kiss. It wasn't long before the two were passionately makin out on the bed forgettin what was outside of the four walls they were in.

The two were makin love under the covers when there was a knock on the front door. Benjamin and Amelia didn't hear the door because they were so wrapped up in each other, and the person outside of the guest house checked the door and found that it wasn't locked so she walked into the house. She quietly made her way through the house until she came to the bedroom door, and when she opened the door enough to where she could see the bed, and her heart was broken because the man she loved was with someone else. Not only was he with someone else but he was with her sister. She watched for a few more minutes and then she yelled, "Benny, how could you do this to me? And with my sister?"

"Reva, how did you get in here?" Benjamin asked, as he turned around to look at her.

"The door was unlocked." Reva explained, as she opened the bedroom door all the way. "Lia, how could you do this to me?"

"You broke up with him." Amelia replied, as she put the cover up over her body as she leaned up against the headboard. "We had just talked about tellin you about us."

"Really?" Reva asked, as she crossed her arms as tears started to fall from her eyes.

"Yes, we did."

"The two of you should be ashamed of yourself. Doin the one thing your grandpa preaches that you shouldn't do because it should be saved for marriage, and the marriage bed shouldn't be defiled."

"We're not perfect." Benjamin explained, as he looked at her very seriously. "We are tempted, and we stumble and fall."

"If your grandpa found out about what the two of you are doin he would kick you out of the church."

"Are you goin to tell him?"

"I might...." Reva explained, as she wiped the tears from her eyes.

"Sis, come on." Amelia said, as she looked at her sister a little scared. "You aren't goin to be that petty are you?"

"I'm sure mom and dad would love to hear that their sixteen-year-old daughter his havin sex with the preacher's grandson."

"Reva, you wouldn't do that to me?"

"Have you grounded for a few months then maybe Benny and I can work our problems out. That sounds like a good idea."

"You wouldn't..?" Amelia said, as she looked at her sister scared of what Reva might do to keep her away from Benjamin.

Austin woke up in a cold sweat straight up in bed not understandin why he would dream somethin like that. He didn't understand why he would be dreamin about Eloise and Jessica, and that the two of them were sisters. As he laid his head back down on the bed and looked up at the cecilin, Austin ran his fingers through his hair and took a deep breath afraid to close his eyes because of what he might dream next.

On Tuesday evenin Austin and Eloise went to Schlatter's Diner for a hamburger and french fries. When they walked into the diner many of the regulars noticed how much Austin looked like the owner's youngest son, and as the regulars started to whisper my mother walked over to the booth and asked, "What do you two youngins what to eat this afternoon?"

"Can we have two cheeseburgers, two fries, and two chocolate milkshakes, please?" Eloise said, crackin a big smile as she handed my mother the menus. My mother cracked a big smile as she took the menus before she walked away. She walked back to the kitchen and yelled the order to the cook. After she was done with that she walked back over to where the other ladies of the diner were standin, and she started watchin Austin and Eloise just like the other ladies.

Just as Austin and Eloise started eatin their dinner when the Roccha's walked into the diner. When the Roccha's made their way to their favorite booth Jessica noticed Austin sittin in the corner booth and she walked over and said, "Austin Reid, what are you doin down here?"

"Hi Jessica, how are you?" Austin replied, as he looked at her crackin his boyish grin. "I came down here to play in a band for the next two weeks."

"I'm good." Jessica said, as she climbed up in the booth beside him.

"What band are you playin with?"

"A band called the Schlatter's, and I'll be playin right here at the diner."

As Jessica picked up a french fry and dipped it into Austin's chocolate shake she said, "Are you goin to spend time with me?"

"Of course, I will.." Austin replied, as his boyish grin turned into a smile.

Mrs. Roccha walked over to the booth where Austin was sittin and said, "Jessica, why don't you let Austin finish eatin his supper."

"Why mama?" Jessica asked, as she took another french fry from Austin's plate.

"I'm sure that Austin and Miss Eloise have somethin to talk about, so why don't you leave them alone and come over to our booth with your father and I."

Jessica finished eatin her french fry and kissed Austin on the cheek before she climbed down from the booth. She walked over with her family's normal booth, and she watched Austin and Eloise from across the room. Her parents watched her wonderin what the fascination still was with Austin even though it had been almost a year since she had seen him. settin up at the counter with the rest of the ladies at the diner was Darlene Schlatter, the owner of the restaurant, and she was blown away by how much Austin looked like her son Benjamin. She also hasn't realized just how much Eloise looked like Reva Roccha who lived on the next farm over from the Schlatter farm. Reva Roccha was a friend of Benjamin's since the two were two years old. She and her sister grew up playin with Benjamin and other kids that lived on the road. Their parents Karla and Kenny Roccha were big cotton farmers, and he was the third-generation farmer in the family.

Back at the booth Austin and Eloise were eatin their supper when Eloise said, "I think that little girl has a crush on you."

"You think so?" Austin asked, before he took a bite of his hamburger crackin his boyish grin.

"Yes, I do."

"So what day are we goin to New York?"

"On Wednesday afternoon because we are goin to the musical on Thursday night."

"So do you have a boyfriend?" Austin asked, as he dipped a french fry into his chocolate milkshake,

"No, I don't. Why?"

"I figured that you would have a lot of guys knockin down your door after you broke up with David."

"There have been a few, but not the boy I wanted." Eloise said, with a big smile as her eyes lit up and she let out a giggle.

After eatin supper Austin and Eloise went back out to Schlatter's farm, and they walked around and explorin the place. Austin and Eloise walked to the edge of the property lookin over at the Roccha farm. They got to know each other as they told stories of their childhood, and what their plans were for the future. As they walked back to their guesthouses Austin put his arm around Eloise's neck, and as the two started to go into deep conversation.

"Would you like to come in for drink?" Eloise asked, as she unlocked and opened her front door.

"Sure, you have liquor in this guesthouse?"

"Yes, I'm very good friends with my parent's limo driver and he buys me anything I want. In fact, we bought liquor for you too."

"You did?"

"Yes, we wanted you to feel at home." Eloise said, as the two walked into the house. She then poured them both a shot of bourbon. "So, is there a special girl back home you're datin?"

"Yes, I have a girlfriend back home." Austin said, as he took a drink from the half full glass of bourbon.

"Damn, I was hopin you didn't."

"Why?"

"Because I've wanted to do this since the time that you got here." Eloise replied, as she set her glass down on the counter and gave him a passionate kiss on the lips.

As Eloise took her lips away from his Austin said, "Wow! I didn't see that one comin."

"I'm sorry.."

"It's all right." Austin said, as he finished drinkin his bourbon.

Eloise took another drink of her bourbon as she looked into his ice blue eyes wonderin what he really thought of her. The two sat down on the couch as they finished their drinks, and then out of the blue Austin leaned over and passionately kissed Eloise. It took Eloise by surprise, but she put her arms around his neck and the two made out on the couch lost in each other's eyes.

On a rainy New York Thursday summer evenin Austin and the girls
had eaten Arturo's restaurant and pizza on one hundred six west Houston
street before they went to Virginia Theatre on W fifty second street to watch
the musical Smokey Joe's Café. Lee Ann, Beverly, Christine, Eloise, and
Austin found their seats right in front of the stage in the middle of the second
row. Eloise was whisperin in Austin's ear as other ticket goers who had seats
in front of them found their seats. Austin looked up as he listened to Eloise
whisper somethin in his ear, and he saw Rosanna, Brittany, Christina,
Margret, and Kelli sittin down in front of him. As the women sat down in their
seats they looked at the crowd that had come to watch the musical. Rosanna
noticed Austin settin behind her. She had an upset look on her face when she
saw Austin flirtin with the girl that was settin beside him. Before she could say
anything to Austin the lights went down, and the announcer said welcomed
the crowd to the one thousand fifty-sixth performance of Smokey Joe's Café.
The spotlights hit the stage as the curtain went up, and the performers
started to Sing the song "In the Neighborhood." When the performers

started to sing the fourth song which the song "Love Me", and then another performer came out onto the stage and started to sing the song "Don't". Tears fell down Austin's face as memories flooded his mind of him and Jessica those two songs together at the talent show at the fair.

In Illinois Jaedyn had talked Jaelyn into goin to a friend's party so that she wouldn't just stay at home the entire time Austin was out of town. Jaedyn really wanted Jaelyn to know that there were other guys out there that would put her first and love her with no one in the middle of them. Jaelyn reluctantly went to the party because she knew her sister wanted her to do things and not sit at home all summer while Austin was on his trip.

Jaelyn was at Reese's party with the liquor flowin, and the teenagers were actin stupid because they were so drunk. Jaelyn was sittin on the couch with a beer in her hand wishin that she hadn't gone to the party. As she set her beer down on the coffee table Remy sat down beside her and said, "How come Austin isn't here with you?"

"He went out of town for a few weeks." Jaelyn replied, as she looked over at him.

"Where did he go?"

"He went to Mississippi."

"Do you trust him?"

"Why wouldn't I trust him." Jaelyn replied, gettin very upset with Remy.

"He's a cute guy." Remy replied, crackin a grin. "And you know that he's always has girls chasin after him."

"I know, but he chose me."

"Then why did he leave town?"

"He's playin in a band, and he's not goin to be with some girl."

"And you believe that?"

"Yes, I do." Jaelyn replied, gettin very defensive.

"Well, I don't believe it." Remy said, in some ways bein really mean. "Austin's probably with another girl right now."

"You're an asshole, Remy. Austin's is goin to be true to me this summer.."

"Well." Remy said, with a smile as he got up from the couch. "If Austin ever breaks your heart I'm here.."

With an upset look on her face Jaelyn reached down for her can of beer and took a drink. As she watched Remy walk away she did wonder if Austin was with another girl at that moment, and was he breakin his promise to her. Would Jaedyn goin to have to end up beatin him up after all.

Back in New York it was intermission time at the musical Austin decided to stay in his seat because he wanted a moment alone from the crowd. Just as he leaned his head back and closed his eyes he heard a sweet New York voice say, "Is this seat taken?"

Austin opened his eyes and saw Rosanna standin beside him and he laughed a little bit because he never thought that he would run into her at that musical out of all the places in New York City. As he cracked his boyish smile he replied, "No, it's not taken you can set down if you want."

"What do you think you're doin with that girl?" Rosanna asked, as she sit down in the chair beside him.

127

"What do you mean?"

"Austin, I'm not blind I saw that girl whisperin in your ear when I set down in my seat before the show. Are you sleepin with her?"

"Why would you ask me that?"

"Are you sleepin with that girl, Austin?"

"No, I haven't slept with her." Austin replied, gettin a little upset that Rosanna would call him out on what he was doin.

"How are you and Jaelyn doin? I noticed that you didn't put anything about her in your last letter to me."

"We're doin all right."

"Just all right?"

"We kind of got in a fight before I left for Mississippi."

"And so you decided to just latch on to the closest girl you could find."

"It's not like that." Austin replied, gettin more upset as the conversation went on. "When I first got to Mississippi and spent the first night in the guesthouse I'm stayin I had a dream."

"What kind of dream?" Rosanna asked, a little curious.

"I dreamed that my name was Benjamin and that I was in love with two sisters. The oldest one looked like the girl who was settin next to me, and the younger one looked like Jessica."

"No way, you're lyin."

"In my dream the older sister and I had broken up and I had started datin the younger one. She wanted us to tell her older sister but I didn't want to. In my dream I was makin love to the younger sister when the older sister came into my house and saw the two of us havin sex." Austin explained, with a scared look on his face. "Then I woke up in a cold sweat scared to death not understanin why I was havin the dream."

"Wow!" Rosanna replied, with a curious look on her face. "But you changed the subject."

"It's been a weird a summer all ready, and I have this feelin that it is only goin to get weirder."

"Have you seen little Jessica and told her that you found the letter in the glovebox."

Just as she said that Rosanna's friends walked back into the theater and Christina said, "Ro, there you are. We've been lookin everywhere for you."

"I ran into an old friend." Rosanna said, with a big smile as she looked over at her.

"Austin Reid, how are you doin?" Brittany said, with a big smile as she sat down in front of him.

"I'm good." Austin replied, crackin his boyish grin.

"What are you doin in NYC?"

"I came with some friends to see the musical."

"That group of girls you are with?"

"Yes, they have a band and want to have a show like this someday."

"Oh." Brittany replied, as she made eyes at him.

"You are Rosanna's friend Austin Reid?" Margret asked, as she sat down in her seat.

"Yes…" Austin replied, knowin who Margret was.

"Ro, he's even cuter in person. I can't believe you let him get away."

"Austin, are you stayin out of trouble?" Kelli asked, with a big smile as she sat down in her seat.

"I'm tryin to, but not havin such good luck on that."

The group were talkin when the other tickets holders started makin their way back into the theater, Rosanna got up out of the chair and made her way to her seat. She was lookin back when she saw the girl who was settin by Austin before givin him a kiss as she sat down beside him. The lights went down and the second half of the musical started.

On Saturday afternoon Austin was walkin around the Schlatter Farm, and he seemed to know where he was goin to get to a certain spot. On his way back to the guesthouse and as he was walkin past the main house when he heard someone on the front porch say, "Child, you look just like Mr. Benjamin who used to live here a long time ago."

Austin stopped walkin, looked up at the front porch, and he saw an elderly black woman swingin on the porch swing enjoyin the afternoon. Wantin to know more about this Benjamin she was talkin about Austin made his way unto the porch and said, "I do. Can you tell me more about him?"

"Of course, I can. Child, find yourself a seat."

"I'm Austin Reid," Austin said, as he reached out his hand and shook her hand as he sat down on the swing beside her.

"Nice to meet you. Everyone calls me Miss Shirley." Shirley said, as she shook his hand. "Mr. Benjamin was Hugo and Darlene' youngest son. He was a spitfire from the moment he came into his world, and he always kept Hugo and Darlene on their toes."

"Really?"

"From the time he was four years old he told his parents he wanted to be a singer in the family group called the Schlatter Quartet. The family were known around here since the thirties because of that singin group traveled all over the south singin in churches all over the country."

"That's the group Christine and Beverly are tryin to bring back to life with the group that they are startin. That's why I'm here this summer to play with them."

"Child, can we go inside this Mississippi heat is gettin to this old lady." Miss Shirley said, as she got up off the swing and started to walk inside.

Austin and Miss Shirely walked inside the house and made their way back to the kitchen. She got Austin a glass of lemonade, and got her scrapbook from her room before she sat down at the table next to him. She opened the book and started flippin through the pages of when Benjamin was a baby to when he was a young boy. Austin couldn't believe how much Benjamin's baby pictures looked just like him when he was a baby, and all the way up to when he was a teenage boy. Miss Shirley turned the page, and the picture was of the Schlatter quartet with Benjamin standin in front of the group with the biggest smile on his face. As she pointed her finger at the picture Mrs. Shirley said, "He was so proud of himself that day his uncles and father came told him that he had been chosen to be in the group after his uncle Roger retired from it."

"Oh, wow! Was he a good singer?

"Oh yes, his father and uncles taught him how sing because the band practices would be at the house in the parlor.. I taught him how to play the piano, and my brother Henry taught him how t play guitar."

"Did his older brothers want to be in the singn group?" Austin asked, bein curious since it was a family group.

"No, not really Mitchell dreamed of bein a preacher when he grew up just just like his grandpa Schlatter. Harold Schlatter was a full Pentecostal preacher, and he preached with hellfire and brimstone. He believed that every word in the bible was true, and that if you even touch any part of the world's temptations you were goin to go to hell. His church was full every Sunday and Wednesday with people who also believed that Jesus is comin back and we all needed to be ready."

"Oh, wow!"

"Now, Elijah, on the other hand, didn't want anything to do with either of the family businesses." Miss Shirley said, with a big smile on her face. he was the black sheep of the family and really had no direction at all. "

"Really?" Austin asked, with a laugh.

"Elijah left Saltillo the day after he graduated from high school. He told his parents that he would write them when he could, but there were many years we heard nothin at all from him."

"So, what happened?"

"Elijah ended up joinin the air force in forty-six and was a fighter pilot for many years. He got to travel around the world and learned many new cultures. In nineteen sixty Elijah retired from the air force, and became a pilot for Pam Am. In early nineteen seventy-five Eljah decided to come home to Saltillo and help Hugo with the farm because all the work was gettin too much for his father. While workin at the farm Elijah met Bridget Logan one day while she was here for a horse ridin lesson. "

"Wow!"

"And in nineteen eighty-one Christine was born." Mrs. Shirley said, with a big smile. "Elijah still helps run the farm with his father."

"So, what happened to Mitchell?"

"Mitchell graduated school in nineteen forty-two, and then he went to Central Bible College in Missouri. After he graduated from Bible college, he came back home and was under the wing of his grandfather for several years. In nineteen seventy-nine Harold Schlatter retired from the ministry, and Mitchell took his position as head of the church. The first couple of months were rough for Mitchell because Harold would cut up his sermon and told him what he could have done to make it better. In nineteen seventy-four Mitchell met Michele Davidson at a church service, and they got married in nineteen seventy-six. and in nineteen eight one Beverly was born."

"Oh boy." Austin said, not surprised that grandpa Schlatter was so very critical of his grandson. "I'm sure that Benjamin was under a lot of pressure with his brother helpin at the farm and his other brother becomin a preacher."

"Yes, but Benny knew what he wanted to do. He wanted to be in the Schlatter quartet, and be the front man for it because he had dreamed of that all his life.." Mrs. Shirley said, as she picked up her coffee cup and took a drink.

.   "The new Schlatter group's first performance is on Sunday at the diner?"

As Austin took his last sip of lemonade and cracked his boyish grin Austin replied, "Yes, it is, and thank you for tellin me about Benjamin, Mrs. Shirley."

On Sunday afternoon Schlatter's Diner had a full crowd of people for lunch, and some left to go do errands that they needed to do before church that night. The rest of the crowd of people waited excitedly for the new Schlatter band to play their first performance. Eloise, Austin, Lee Ann. Beverly, and Christine made their way over to the instruments that were set up in the corner of the restaurant. As those playin guitars strapped their instruments on Beverly stepped up to the microphone and said, "Good after-noon, first all of us want to thank you for you for comin to see us today. As you know mine and Christine's family as a legacy of music in this town, and although we don't know all about it we wanted to continue that legacy.

This is our first performance live with our friend Austin Reid, so you may have to bear with us as we stumble through a few of the songs."

"Of course, she's goin to blame it on me." Austin said, crackin his boyish grin as he stepped up to his microphone.

The crowd got a big laugh out of what Austin had said, and Beverly counted down and the band started to play their first song. In the audience both both Elijah and Mitchell watched their daughters and couldn't believe how good that they were. The two men were so proud of them for wantin to keep the family's legacy alive. Also in the audience was the Roccha family sittin at their normal booth, and Mr. and Mrs. Roccha watched their daughter Jessica wear a big smile as she watched Austin perform..

An hour and a half later the Schlatter's sung their final song which was "Amazin Grace." As the band members started tearin down their equipment, people from the crowd started walkin up to the corner, and tellin them just how much they loved the performance. Many people told them that if they closed their eyes they could see the original Schlatter's standin there singin, and proud they would be of them for what they are doin. Austin had just set his guitar in his case when Jessica ran up to him, and gave him the biggest hug she could. With a big smile Jessica said, "You were so good, sunshine."

"Well, thank you." Austin replied, as he looked at her crackin his boyish grin. "I'm glad you liked it, Jessica."

"Why do you call him sunshine, Jessica?" Beverly asked, just bein nosy as she put her guitar in its case.

"I've always called him sunshine." Jessica explained, getting upset.

"Is that your nickname for him?"

"Yes, it is.."

"Why do you call him that?" Lee Ann asked, just curious what the answer would be.

"Because is smile is like the sunshine."

"Really?" Christine asked, with a laugh as she looked at the little girl.

"Yes. His smile always brightens up my day."

"Ok." Eloise said, with a smile and laugh. "It brightens up my day too."

Jessica looked at the girls with the most unhappy stare because she couldn't understand why they would make fun of her callin Austin sunshine. After a few minutes she stomped away back to where her parents were at, and as the family left to go back home Jessica waved at Austin and he waved back.

Up in Illinois Reese, Peyton, Hope, Maddy, Jaedyn, Jaelyn, and a few others were at Reese's house eatin supper at the kitchen table since they were havin a girl's night. As she took a bite of her pancakes Maddy asked, "Where is Austin this summer, Jaelyn?"

"He went to Mississippi to play in a band for a couple of weeks." Jaelyn replied, as she put more syrup on her pancakes.

"The same place he and Lane went to last year?" Peyton asked, as she looked over at Jaelyn just bein nosy.

"Yes."

"Do you trust him?" Hope asked, as she took a drink of her orange juice.

"Is there a girl involved in this band that is in playin in?" Eileen asked, also bein nosy.

"Yes, I think so." Jaelyn replied, as she took a bite of her pancakes.

"You may have your heart broke by the end of the summer." Hope said bein very blunt about what she thought.

"She's right." Peyton replied, with a very serious look on her face.

"I'm sure he's probably already had sex with that girl since you wouldn't do it with him." Reese said, makin Jaelyn only worry more about her relationship with Austin.

"You think so?"

"Yes…" All the girls said, at the same time.

"Sis, don't listen to them." Jaedyn said, speakin up. "They have no clue what Austin is doin, and you need to trust that he will be faithful to you because you know that he loves you."

"I know.." Jaelyn said, as she moved a piece of pancake around with her fork. "And I wanted to before he left, but he said I wasn't ready."

141

"You did what?" Eileen said shocked, as she cut another piece of pancake to eat.

"I asked him to make love to me before he left for Mississippi, but he wouldn't do it."

"Wow!." Maddy said, a little surprised by Jaelyn's answer.

"Wow! I can't believe that you did that, J." Reese explained, very shocked by Jaelyn's answer

"He must hold you in high regard like he did Jessica." Hope said, just addin salt to the wound she knew Jaelyn had about Jessica.

"You think so?"

"The question is who will he turn to since he said that you're not ready." Peyton asked, crackin a grin as she drank her milk.

"I know." Jaelyn replied, as her mind wondered thinkin what Austin was doin in that moment..

"Don't do that.." Jaedyn said, knowin what her friends were doin. "Don't make her worry more just to make yourself feel good."

"We're not.." Reese said, crackin a big smile.

"We're just lettin her know the score." Peyton said, takin another bite of her food.

"I do wonder who he's hangin around right now."

"Jaelyn, don't listen to them." Jaedyn said, knowin that they were only tryin to get Austin and Jaelyn apart so that Reese could have another shot at him.

"I am worried because he hasn't called me at all since he left town." Jaelyn said, with a very worried look on her face.

For Lane the summer was like any other summer she had grownin up. She played summer softball at the park, but she was workin a summer job at her dad's place of work. She was savin every check because she wanted to buy her aunt's car, but she was goin to spend one of two when the Georgetown Fair came to town. She was happy that the guys in the maintenance department at her dad's place of work were nice and welcomed her with open arms. Still, with the two people she was workin alongside she felt very small and insignificant since they both had big personalities.

That summer Lane learned more about her aunt Denise from her grandma
and grandpa Sutton. She learned that she was a vibrant little girl with dreams
dreams of becomin a nurse when she got older. She watched out her two
younger siblins, and made sure that they were taken care of when her mama
and daddy were busy with adult things. She was just learnin how to cook
from Grandma Sutton, and one of the first things she learned to make was
chocolate gravy. It was a recipe that Grandma Sutton had grown up eatin
when she was a young girl. Great grandma Harrelson had taught her to
make it when she lived with her when she was growin up. Denise loved to
eat chocolate gravy with biscuits, a little butter, and the gravy on top of it.

One evenin after she had got home from work Lane was sittin on the
bed when she thought a few lines for a song, but she didn't write her a
thoughts down and she quickly forgot them. The next few days those lines
came back to her with a bunch of new lines, and it percolated in her mind for
a few more days. Then one evenin she grabbed a notebook and a pencil

As she wrote these words on a piece of paper.

I'm stumblin to heaven

Yes, I'm stumblin to heaven

Through every trial and tribulation

(Walkin through every storm)

Slowly stumblin my way to the joys of heaven

But, I'm stumblin (Oh, yes)

I'm stumblin to heaven

Born in the shadow of someone else

I worked hard to make a success of myself

Not wantin to put my life on a shelf

Unsurely made it through the hand I was dealt

Moving forward in spite of everyone else

Slowly findin strength within myself

Believin each step was the right one

I wouldn't listen to anyone

Knowin it seemed to everyone

I'd lost my chance to start over again

Didn't expect to hear the lord to say "Well done"

Even if it was a gospel song I sung

It's never easy to come to a crossroad

Choosin to live the way I was told

Or believin the devil would carry my heavy load

I'm stumblin to heaven

Yes, I'm stumblin to heaven

Through every trial and tribulation

(Walkin through every storm)

Slowly stumblin my way to the joys of heaven

But, I'm stumblin (Oh, yes)

I'm stumblin to heaven

After she wrote those words Lane started to think about how her mother was always in the shadow of Denise, and how Lane's own sister was in the shadow of her because of her deformity. She realized even in herself that she was stumblin to heaven because she wasn't perfect and stumbled many times because of what the world had done to her. She was relyin on things of this world to take her pain away and not confront the fear that was in front of her. In Lane's mind she would rather check out than overcome the obstacle in front of her because she thought she wasn't strong enough to do it

Sunday mornin in Mississippi around ten o' clock me and my family were in our normal seats at church. Austin was singin and playin the mornin hymns with the girls, and in the pew Jessica was standin up watchin Austin with the biggest smile on her face. Once the hymns were sung Austin and the girls sat down in their seats in the pews, and Rev. Schlatter walked up to the podium and said, "Today I would like to read from the book of Jonah. The lord had called him to do a great task, and asked him to go to Niveah to call out the evil in that city. What did Jonah do?"

"He ran away." A fragile skinny elderly woman yelled, sittin in the middle of church.

"Yes, he did run away. Jonah went to Tarshish to get away from the presence of the lord, but the presence of the lord went with Jonah."

"Oh, come on now." An elderly man settin by that elderly woman said, loudly.

"The lord brought a great wind upon see that threatened the ship that Jonah was on. All the crew and passengers were afraid and many cried out to God to help them. They began to throw things overboard so that the ship was light and wouldn't sink. In the inner part of the ship Jonah had laid down and fell asleep, and the captain went down to wake him up askin him to call out to his god to help him."

148

"That's it, preach it." Mr. Schlatter yelled, from the front row.

"The people on board cast lots to see who was causin the evil on the ship, and the lot fell on Jonah. They asked him to explain himself and he told them that he was a Hebrew and that he feared the lord. Then the men asked him what they could so that the sea would quiet down for them. Jonah told them to pick him up and threw him overboard, but they decided to row toward the dry land as the sea grew rougher against them. After cryin out to God they picked Jonah up and threw him overboard, and the sea calmed down and then they offered sacrifice to God and made vows."

"Preach it, Rev." A heavy-set middle-aged man said, yellin from the back row.

"Before Jonah to catch his breath he was swallowed by a great fish, and he was in the belly of that fish." Rev. Schlatter said, as he wiped his forehead off with his handkerchief. "The boy was lost because he didn't know what to do now, so he did what he knew to do in other great times of fear. Jonah prayed to the lord while in the belly of that fish. In his prayer he prayed about what he had been through and what the lord had done for him. He was also thankful for what the lord had done for him in the past and what he was about to do for him at that moment the fish didn't vomit him up in the ocean where he would have to swim to reach the dry land, but God told the fish to vomit him up on dry land where his feet would be firmly planted without stumbling or fallin."

"Oh. come on!"

"Let's go, Rev." A middle-aged blonde headed woman said, from the the middle of row.

"Jonah went to Nineveh the great city, and while he was there he called out that the city would be overthrown in forty days. The word reached the king of the city he set in ashes and sackcloth, and he asked the people of the city to turn from their evil ways.."

"Preach it."

"When God saw what the people of the city he did not destroy the city which made Jonah mad. After he went out of the city he was upset that god didn't destroy the city, and why would he go all the way to there for them to be saved. Then the lord shaded him, and then killed the plant, and Jonah then wanted to die, but then the lord talked to him about why he had to save

150

the people because they did what he had asked of them to do." Rev. Schlatter said, as he closed his bible and looked at his congregation. "So, what is the moral of this story about Jonah?"

"Follow the lord instructions.." That blonde-haired middle-aged woman yelled, from the middle of the church.

"Amen." Many people from the congregation yelled, with smiles as they looked at each other.

"Yes, that is true we all need to follow the instructions the lord gives us." Rev. Schlatter said, with a little giggle. "But there is more to it than that."

"Tell us, Rev." A tall skinny dark-haired teenage boy yelled, with a big grin.

"We all have a purpose on this earth to fulfill, and some of us find it very early in life. Others have to search for it when they don't realize that their purpose on the earth can be found in their hearts. We just have listen to our hearts to find our purpose on the earth."

"Oh, yea. Preach it!"

"Think about what you love to do and then think about if you want to do it for the rest of your life."

Settin in the pew Austin thought about what the preacher was sayin, and realized that he had always dreamed of bein on a stage since he was little. Austin really hadn't thought about his impact on the world when he was older and on that stage in front of a million or so people. He also thou about his impact if he ever got into the movies or on television. He then started to wonder what Benjamin's impact on the world was durin his time on the earth.

"When God gives you an assignment you don't run away from it." Rev. Schlatter replied, as he wiped his forehead with his handkerchief. "Embrace that callin that God has given you and take it to the world to inspire strangers."

"Preach it, Rev.."

"Just one word from you can change a person's life in ways that you never thought it could." Rev. Schlatter said, with a big smile. "So, when you come across someone, and get into a conversation with them think before you speak. Make sure that your words cheer them up and not tear them down because what we do has a ripple effect on the society that we live in."

Rev. Schlatter talked for another twenty minutes before he said the prayer at the end of the service. The quiet was shattered when the people in the congregation started talkin about the latest gossip they had heard at the diner durin the week. It was no surprise that Jessica Roccha ran over to say hi to Austin after the service was over, and her parents weren't that far behind her Austin and the Roccha's talked for a good ten minutes, and Jessica wanted all his attention.

On Tuesday evenin Austin went up to the main house to visit with Miss Shirley. As the two snacked on coffee and cookies Miss Shirley got out her Scrapbook. She showed him pictures of Benjamin and the neighbor girls that he grew up with. As Austin looked at the pictures with Benjamin and the neighbor girls, he noticed that one looked like Eloise and the other one looked like Jessica. After catchin his breath he said, "I had a dream the first night I got here, and it was about Benjamin datin the younger girl. He and the older sister had broken up, but he didn't want to tell her that he was datin her.

sister. Then the older sister walked in and found them together."

"Oh, yes." Mrs. Shirley said, as she looked at the picture. "Benny, went out with miss Reva Roccha for years as they grew up together. Her younger sister Amelia was always hangin around them when they were on the farm or on their farm. Benjamin never paid that much attention to Ameila until his senior year and her sophomore year of high school."

"So was Benjamin in love with Amelia, or did he love Reva more?"

"That boy fell head over heels in love with Amelia. They had a love like no other I've ever seen in my life. Benjamin and Amelia shared everything with each other, and were so close that you would have thought they were one person."

"That sounds like my relationship with my girlfriend Jessica." Austin said, as he got his wallet out of his pants and took a picture of the two of them out of it. "We were so close and fell in love with each other at a young age."

Mrs. Shirley looked at the picture and her mouth dropped as she looked down at the picture of Benjamin and Amelia. As she sat back in the chair she said, "Child, do you know that you and your girlfriend look just like Benjamin and Amelia?"

"Yes, ma' am, I did notice that."

"I feel like I'm in the twilight zone because this is just unreal to me. How much you look like Benny, and the people in your life look like the ones in his life."

"Have you ever heard of reincarnation, and that we live many lives on the earth?" Austin asked, as he took the picture back.

"Yes, I have seen on the news, but I didn't believe in it because of what I was taught at church." Miss. Shirley replied, still in shock over how much Austin looked like Benjamin. "And how is your girlfriend are you goin to tell her about this?"

"Oh, Jessica was kidnapped and killed back in nineteen ninety-three When I was twelve years old"

"I'm sorry, dear."

"But my cousin and I are both learnin about past lives and what are our journey is on the earth." Austin replied, as he wiped the tears from his eyes. "And this is very interestin to me to think that maybe we both were on the earth before and were together in that life too."

"Benjamin and Amelia had their lives all planned out by the time it was time for him to graduate in the spring of nineteen sixty-five." Mrs. Shirley said, as she turned the scrapbook to the next page.

"What was that?"

"Benjamin got drafted into the army, and he had to show up just a few days after graduation."

Austin looked down at the draft notice and could see the faint tear stains on it and as he looked up at her he said, "Well, there wasn't any war so he would only be in for a few years and then get out right?"

"The war in Vietnam started in nineteen fifty-five, but the American's didn't really have troops over there until nineteen sixty-one. Amelia was heart sick when she learned that Benjamin had been drafted into the army because she felt that somethin bad was goin to happen to him and the two wouldn't be together."

"So, what happened to Benjamin?" Austin asked, as he turned the page of the scrapbook and saw in him his green fatigues.

"The night before he left for basic trainin at Ft. Knox in Kentucky he gave Amelia his high school ring because he couldn't afford to buy her an engagement ring. He wrote to me, Amelia, and his family not long after he got there. He told me that he didn't like it at all because the people in charge would try to break your spirit, so that they could mold him into bein the soldier that he needed to be."

"I bet.." Austin said, thinkin about how bad it would be to just be summoned to an unfamiliar place with strangers and all they did was yell at you.

"It wasn't long after basic trainin that he got ship to Vietnam."

"What did his family think about him goin to Vietnam?"

"They were proud of him because they believed that it was his duty when called upon by Uncle Sam that you stand and fight whomever is threatenin someone's freedom." Ms. Shirley said, as she picked up her cup of coffee.

"Did he write her a lot once he was shipped over there?"

"Oh, yes. That boy sent five or six letters a week. He kept reassurin her that he would be comin back and the two would get married in his grandfather's church."

"Wow!" Austin said, crackin a smile as he looked at the pictures of Benjamin in Vietnam. "Most men would probably cheat on their girlfriend so many miles away."

"I think that he may have because when they showed pictures on the television screen there were always girls on the base with the men. In the spring of nineteen sixty-seven Benjamin's letters stopped, and everyone started to get scared thinkin about what might have happened to him."

"So, what did happen to him?"

"His parents received a letter tellin them that he had been wounded in the battle of Ap Gu in Ninh Province. He was taken to the medical ship, and then taken to the Letterman hospital in San Fransico, California. I can't tell you how happy everyone was to get the news, and they couldn't wait until he returned home."

"Was he injured very badly?" Austin asked, as he turned the page in the scrapbook.

"He had been shot in the left shoulder and in the right leg. That is where he met Dakota Burke She was a nurse at the hospital and helped him recover from his wounds. He told me that she would make him smile every day as the two talked for hours every day about everything and nothin at all."

"How long was in the hospital?"

"He was there for about three months, and then when he left the hospital he stayed with Dakota because San Fransico was the place to be. Everyone was makin their way out there because it had become the place for counterculture for the norms of society."

"Oh yea, I remember learnin about that in history class too. It was the hippie generation wasn't it?"

"Yes. As spring turned into to summer in San Fransico also came the summer of love. While Dakota was at work Benjamin would walk around town seein what all the city had to offer. He spent many days in Haight-Ashbury and over time Benjamin became a hippie just like the people he was hangin out with. He had encountered marijuana in the army over in

Vietnam, but his taste for harder drugs started while he was in San Fransico. At that time in the music world Janis Joplin and Big Brother Holdin Company were catchin fire along with the Grateful Dead, Buffalo Springfield, and other music groups. Dakota was upset with Benjamin when he started to do the harder drugs. She tried to get him to stop takin them, but it was a fight that she wasn't goin to win."

"Oh, wow." Austin said, very surprised that Benjamin would go so deep into drug use.

"Did Benjamin ever come home to see his family?"

"Yes, he did." Miss. Shirley said, with a big smile as she turned the page. "It was the Christmas of nineteen sixty-eight. When I opened the front door I didn't recognize him at first because his hair was grown out to his shoulders, he had a beard, and he was wearin sunglasses. I was curious when I saw that there was a dark-haired woman standin next to him and the two were holdin hands."

"Were his parents happy to see him?"

"Yes, there were very happy to see him, but they didn't like his new attitude.. They were just as shocked as I was when they met Dakota for

160

the first time because they thought that he was goin to marry Amelia."

"What was Amelia's reaction when she saw him?"

"When Amelia saw him that first Sunday in church she was happy that he had made it home alive because of the news reports of American's dyin over there. She was very heartbroken, but she knew that it was because of what her parents made her do."

"So, when did all the good stuff happen between the three of them?" Austin asked, as he looked down at the picture she was talkin about and couldn't believe his eyes. The woman standin next to Benjamin in the picture looked just like Rosanna. Austin couldn't get over the feelin of havin déjà vu because it seemed like all the women he knew in his life were in were also in Benjamin's life.

"That another story for another time." Miss Shirley said, with a big laugh. "You need to do some diggin on your own in the house to see what you can find before I tell you anything else."

Later that evenin Austin thought about what Mrs. Shirley had told him and the pictures he had seen. The next thought was how could it be related to his life now, and what was he on the earth to learn. After tossin and turnin for a few hours, Austin finally fell asleep and went off to dreamland. Around four o' clock in the mornin Austin was in his bedroom soundly sleepin in bed when in his dream he looked over at the doorway and saw Jessica standin there. As he leaned up against the bed he said, "Have we been together in more lives than just the one we're livin right now?"

"Yes, sunshine." Jessica said, crackin a big smile. "We've have been together in multiple lives."

"Are we goin to have a good life in this life too?"

"I believe that we will when the time comes for us to be together again." Jessica replied, as she walked over from the doorway and sat down on the bed beside him.

"I can't wait." Austin said, as he pulled her closer to him.

Jessica just cracked a big smile as she gave him a kiss and started to tickle him. She knew right where his tickle spots were, so it soon became a tickle fight as they tickled each other. The next thing Austin knew the tickle fight turned into a pillow fight as Jessica took one of the pillows off the bed and started to hit him with it. Austin then grabbed a pillow of his own and started to hit Jessica with it.

At the house next door Jessica was sleepin in her bed with a big smile on her face. Mrs. Roccha had gotten up to check on her daughter because unlike many times durin the week Jessica hadn't gotten up runnin to their room havin a bad dream. Her mother wondered what her daughter was dreamin about that could put that big of a smile on her face. She stood there and watched Jessica for a few minutes before she walked back to her room.

Up in Illinois Lane was still researchin past lives and how you could Remember your own. She had found a relaxation technique and words to say, so that nigh so as she laid down for bed she said those words, of course, she didn't expect anything to happen after she had said them out loud. After lyin there for about two hours she finally went to sleep around four o' clock.

that mornin, she was sound asleep and off in dreamland. She found herself turnin a hotel room key in the door and openin it. As she walked into the room she noticed the décor of the hotel she could tell that it was back in the thirties or forties. Lane was shuttin the door when she felt two arms go around her waist and two lips kissin her neck. As she enjoyed the moment the guy kissin her said, "How come it took you so long to get here?"

"My father was askin too many questions, Dylan." Lane replied, as she just enjoyed the feelin of an older man wantin her.

"What could he possibly be askin you?" Dylan asked, as he kissed her on her neck.

"Where I was goin, who I was meetin, and when was he goin to meet this new boyfriend of mine."

"What did you say?"

"I told him that I was just meetin some friends at a restaurant close to the ocean, and that I would be back before midnight. How did you get out of the house away from your wife and daughters?"

"I told them I had some errands to run, and that I would be home later." Dylan explained, crackin a big smile. "Why don't you move out and get a place of your own?"

"I can't." Lane replied, as she turned around and looked into his big blue eyes. "I promised my sisters that I would stay at home until Rose graduated and we would all move out together."

"Can't you change your promise for me?"

"You know that I can't do that."

"Maybe I need to find us a place."

"That would be a better option." Lane said, as she kissed him. "But how are you goin to do that without your wife findin out?"

"I'll put it in your name, but I will pay all the bills." Dylan said, with a big smile. "Or we can split the bills? It's whatever you want to do."

Lane turned over in the bed and opened her eyes feelin very over-whelmed. The dream felt so real like a memory she had forgotten but she felt the love that Dylan had for her. She began to wonder if it was just her imagination because she liked Mr. Somerled, and the only way she could be with him was in her dreams.

165

Still, she couldn't get over the fact that it felt so real, and the two were so in love with each other even with all the circumstances keep them apart.

On Saturday afternoon everyone went to Schlatter's diner for catfish, Austin was there eatin with the Roccha's that evenin after spendin the day with them Jessica was so happy because Austin had spent the day with her, and she was the focus of all his attention that day. A huge thunderstorm quickly rolled through Saltillo as Austin got seconds on catfish and fries, Austin walked back over and sat down beside Jessica. As he dipped his french fry into his milkshake Jessica took it away and ate it quickly. With a big laugh and smile Austin asked, "Why did you do that?"

"Because I wanted to" Jesssica replied, with a big smile and laugh as she took another fry off of his plate.

"All you had to do was ask, and I would have given it to you."

"It's more fun takin it away from you."

Austin just looked at Jessica with a big smile and as he remembered all the many times his Jessica did that when they were growin up. He remembered the big smile she always had, and her laugh was like a melody that he could never forget. After he caught his breath Austin asked, "So this is what I have to look forward to when you get older?"

"Yep!" Jesscia said, with a big smile and giggle as she ate the other french fry she had taken.

"I'm sorry I haven't you written you any letters. My life got a little complicated, and I didn't find any time to do it."

"It's alright. Just start writin to me when you go home this time, sunshine."

"Ok, I will make you sure that I find to do this time."

"Did you find those three things I told you about the last time you were here?"

"Yes, I did. And they were right where you told they would be."

"So you know the truth don't you?" Jessica said, as her eyes lit up before she gave him a hug.

"Yes, I do." Austin said, as he gave her a bear hug knowin that he was holdin his Jessica and that she would be in his life from that moment on.

Mr. and Mrs. Roccha looked at each other knowin exactly what Austin and their daughter were talkin about. They still couldn't believe that he had found the things Jessica had told him about last summer. In that moment, Mr. and Mrs. Roocha knew that Austin would be in their lives forever because of what findin those three things meant. They also knew that Jessica wanted Austin to be in her life forever because she seemed to care so much for him even though she was only three years old.

A few feet away Eloise was watchin Austin and Jessica, and she was jealous of the little girl gettin so much of Austin's time and attention. As Beverly turned around to say somethin to Eloise, she noticed the upset look on her face and asked, "E, what's the matter?"

With a disgusted look on her face as she crossed her arms Eloise said, "I thought after comin back from New York Austin and I would spend a lot of time together, but he seems to make more time for that little girl."

"You're jealous of a three-year-old?"

"Yes."

"Have you even made out with him yet?"

"Yes, after he first got down here.." Eloise said, as she crossed her hands.

"Eloise, if somethin is meant to happen between the two of you it will." Beverly said, crackin a big smile. "Besides, he's goin to be a member of our band, so you'll have a lifetime to chase after him."

"I sure hope that you're right." Eloise replied, as she looked over at Austin still very jealous.

A few days later Miss Shirley gave him the key to get into Benjamin's House so that he could look around. She wanted him to look around and

Find things on his own since he looked so much like Benjamin. He started lookin in the nightstand by the bed, but the top drawer didn't have anything in it. When he moved to the second drawer he found a scrapbook, so he decided to get it out and look at it. As he turned the pages the book reminded him of the scrapbook that he and Jessica had started. There were pictures of Benjamin and Amelia when they were little along with other pictures as they grew up. When he turned to the middle of the scrapbook he found that the two had written their weddin vows to each other when they were kids just like he and Jessica had years ago. He turned the page and there was a picture of Benjamin and Amelia after he had come back from Vietnam. Austin closed his eyes and as he laid back on the pillow and the memory of that day came into focus. It was a stormy Saturday evenin and Benjamin was sittin on the couch listenin to his records and drinkin beer along with hard liquor. Dakota was workin the late shift at Tupelo Hospital, and Benjamin was home alone. He had just opened another beer when there was a knock on the door, so he stumbled to the door and answered it. A smile came across his face when she saw who standin in front of him and said, "Lia, how are you doin?"

"I'm good, Benny." Amelia said, lookin into Benny's eyes and seein that he was so lost.

"Come in and have a seat."

Amelia walked into the little house and saw pictures of Benjamin and Dakota all over the walls, and she was jealous because it should have been her and Benjamin's pictures on the walls. As she sat down on the couch Amela said, "Benny, I'm worried about you."

"Lia, why are you worried about me?"

"Since Vietnam you aren't the same lovin guy that you were before, and I'm afraid that I'll never see that guy again."

"War changed me, Lia." Benjamin said, as he sat down on the couch beside her. "When you see women and children gettin shot, and your friends dyin around you it changes you."

"I will never understand how the Vietnam war affect you, but I want to help you find that loveable guy you were before."

"Angel eyes, I don't know if I'll ever be that loveable guy again." Benjamin said, as he looked into Amelia's eyes seein the love she still had him.

"Do you think we can find our way back to each other?"

"I don't know.. I've gone down a rabbit hole I don't think that I will ever find my way out of."

"Benny, let me help you." Ameilia said, as she leaned over and kissed him on the lips.

Benjamin just smiled as he put his arms around her and pulled her closer to him. The two made out on the couch for quite some time, and as they started to make their way to the bedroom clothes began to come off. As they got to the doorway of the bedroom Benjamin pushed Ameila up to it and passionately kissed her. Amelia started to unbutton his pants as the two made their way over to the bed and fell on it, and then the two passionately made out on the bed.

Up in Illinois Lane was still a little confused by the dream she had the week before, and she didn't know what it meant. She did some more research about past lives, and how souls reconnect with each other when they are on the earth. At that point in her life Lane didn't even love herself so how could she love someone else. Lane also believed that Mr. Somerled was happily married, and if she was brave enough to tell him how she felt he might laugh in her face. Plus, the divorce of her parents was still so fresh

172

and present in her life, and Lane didn't want to cause that kind of harm to anyone else. She did start to talk to the lord about why was this happenin to her,and what it was that she had to learn from it. Lane seemed to be left with more questions than answers at this point in her life, and she just wanted to know how all the puzzle pieces fit into her life.

That night she had gone to bed wonderin if she would remember anything else, or if that memory would be the only one that she remembered. she was sleepin soundly when in the dream she was standin in front of French doors lookin outside as the ocean waves roll In and out, and as she smelled the salty air two arm wrapped around her waist and a familiar voice asked, "So do you love our house by the sea?"

"Yes, Dylan, I do." Lane said, with a smile as she put her hand on his. "I still can't believe that you bought this house in Malibu."

"This place is perfect for us." Dylan said, as he kissed hissed on the neck.

"I still don't know how you did this without your wife findin out about it."

"I told the guy at the bank that I was helpin a friend out, and it needed to stay between the two of us."

"I sure hope that he doesn't talk." Lane said, as she turned around and gave him a kiss.

"You just have to go with me to the bank and sign the papers and the place will be ours."

"When do I need to do that?"

"On Wednesday afternoon." Dylan replied, crackin a big smile. "I know that you don't work on Wednesday, and with school gettin out early I thought we could do it around two o' clock."

"Ok, sounds good to me."

Dylan took her hand and led her through the livin room to the kitchen, and showin her that it had all the amenities she needed if she ever wanted to cook. Then he led her down the hall showin her the bathroom and the extra bedrooms and then led her to the master bedroom. As Lane walked in and looked around she thought about how it would feel like if he came home every day to her, and the two ended every night in their bedroom.

"I think I'm goin to like it here." Lane said, crackin a smile as she looked over at him.

"I think I will too." Dylan said, as he walked into the room puttin his arms around her waist.

"I can't believe that you did this.."

"Sweet baby, you know that I would do anything for you."

"You are somethin else, teddy bear." Lane said, as she put her arms arms around his neck and kissed him.

"I think we need to try out the new bed." Dylan said, as he kissed her on the nose.

Lane cracked a little grin as she kissed as the two started walkin over to the bed. As the two fell back on the bed they both laughed before gettin lost in each other's eyes for the next few hours.

Lane opened her eyes and smiled as she remembered that memory because of the smell of the ocean water. She started to realize that she and Mr. Somerled had been in a past life together, and that was why his spirit seemed so familiar to her. As Lane stared at the cecilin she wondered if Mr. Somerled recognized her soul like she was startin to recognize his, and would they end up makin their way back to each other in the present life they were livin in.

Back in Saltillo Austin was lost in his dream as he made love to Amelia, and everything seemed to be right in his life once again. After Benjamin and Amelia made love, the two were under the sheets just starin at each other so happy with what had just happened between them. Breakin the silence Amelia said, "Benny, I love you."

"I love you, Amelia." Benjamin said, as he kissed on the forehead. "How did we get so far away from each other?"

"Life got in the way."

"Are you goin to marry Jeffery?"

As Amelia looked at the diamond engagement ring on her left hand she said, "I don't love him, and I only went out with him to make my parents happy. I won't marry him if you say we have another chance."

176

"Don't marry him, Amelia. Let's give our love story another chance."

"Really?" Amelia said, crackin a grin as she looked into Benjamin's blue eyes.

"Yes." Benjamin replied, givin her a passionate kiss on the lips.

Outside of the guesthouse Dakota had come home early because she hadn't gotten sick while she was workin. She found it odd that the bedroom light was on in the house because when she had left for work Benjamin was in the livin room drinkin and listenin to his favorite records. She got out of the car and slammed the door, but inside Ameila and Benjamin were so into each other that they didn't hear the car door slam. Dakota made her way onto the porch, and as she went to unlock the door she found that it just opened by itself She walked in lookin around to see if Benjamin was all right, and as she made her way into the house she saw Benjamin makin love to someone else on the bed that they shared. Dakota stormed into the bedroom and yelled, "Benjamin, what the hell is goin on here?"

"Dakota, what are you doin home?" Benjamin said, as he quit kissin Amelia and looked over at the bedroom door.

"I got sick at work, and they sent me home." Dakota explained, as she held back the tears she wanted to cry. "You son of a bitch, how could you

177

do this to me again?"

Amelia started to put her clothes on and when she was done she quickly walked out of the room. Benjamin watched Amelia leave and then looked at Dakota and said, "I'm sorry…This is the first and only time it's happened."

"That doesn't matter. It should never have happened if you love me like you say you do."

"I was drunk and the two of us reminiscin about the past." Benjamin said, as he put on his boxer shorts. "I guess, I just longed for the past in the moment. I'm sorry, it won't happen again."

"You're damn right it won't happen again." Dakota said, as she walked to the closet and got her suitcase. "I'm goin back to California."

"Why?"

"Because I know that this will only happen again and again."

"No, it won't." Benjamin said, as he tried to stop her from puttin her clothes in the suitcase.

"I know it will." Dakota said, as tears streamed down her face. "Because I see the way you look at her, and you never look that way at me."

"Can you just sit down so we can talk about this." Benjamin said, as he sat down on the edge of the bed.

"There's nothin to talk about because I just kept your bed warm until you got back together you're with your precious Amelia."

"Dakota, I love you. Stay so we can work this out." Benjamin said, as tears started streamin down his face.

"I'm leavin tonight." Dakota said, as she got the last of her stuff together and headed for the front door.

After puttin her things into her car Dakota peeled out of the driveway in a cloud of dust, leavin Benjamin standin on the porch in his boxer shorts knownin that he had messed up pretty bad. Once the dust cleared Benjamin made his way back into the house, he grabbed the six pack of beer out of the fridge and made his way back to the bedroom where he drank himself to sleep that night. Austin woke up in a cold sweat straight up in the bed. He shook his head as he ran his finger through his hair. As he looked around the bedroom, he could feel that what he had dreamed was very real and that it happened He did start to wonder how many times Benjamin had cheated on

Dakota while they were in California, and why Dakota was hell bent on leavin him not givin him a second chance.

On a hot muggy rainy Tuesday afternoon Austin had gone upto the main house to visit Miss Shirley, and try to get her to tell him what had happened between Benjamin, Amelia, and Dakota. Because he kept havin that same dream over and over when Dakota would come into the bedroom and catch him with Amelia. Austin sat down at the table and started helpin Miss Shirley peel potatoes and said, "Ok, I think it's time you tell me what happened with Benjamin, Amelia, and Dakota because I leave town next Sunday to go back home to Illinois."

"Ok, Mr. Austin." Miss Shirley said, crackin a big smile as she peeled the skin from a potato.

"After Benny and Dakota moved to Saltillo from California Miss Dakota saw the friendship that Benny and Miss Amelia had. Even though Miss Ameila was engaged to Mr. Jeffery Miss Dakota could saw the way Miss Ameila and Benny looked at each other when they were in the same room."

"Who was this Jeffery guy?" Austin asked as he picked a potato up to peel.

"Where did Amelia meet him at?"

"Mr. Jeffery is Jeffery Higgins of the Higgins Farms down the road. His family farm was big in both cotton and rice."

"Oh, ok."

"They made big money just like the other farms in the Mississippi, and once Benjamin had left for the army Mr. Jeffery started makin his moves on Miss Amelia. He would always come to the diner and have lunch just so he could talk to her, but he knew that she was in love with Benjamin. After her parents told her that she couldn't see Benjamin anymore, Amelia started datin Mr. Jeffery about four months later but I could tell that she wasn't happy. I was really surprised when we found out that she said yes to marryin him because I knew that her heart still belonged to Benjamin. When Benjamin finally came home and brought Miss Dakota with him, it seemed like Ms. Amelia was goin to marry Mr. Jeffery just to make Benny jealous."

"Wow!" Austin said, surprised by what had happened after Benjamin had come home to Saltillo.

"Mr. Jeffery was Benny's best friend since they were little boys, and Benny was upset when he and Dakota went to church, and he saw Amelia walk holdin hands with his best friend."

"Oh, boy."

"It was a hot muggy stormy night, and the rain was pourin down in buckets outside. From what can remember Miss. Amelia had come over to visit with Benny because she had become worried about him after seein him at church one Sunday mornin. She wasn't surprised to find him playin his music loud and havin a beer in his hand because he had done it since he was a teenager."

"So there was definitely still feelins still between them?"

"Oh yes, anyone who looked at Miss Amelia and Benny could still see the love they had for each other in their eyes whenever they were lookin at each other. But that night Miss Dakota came home early from work because she had gotten sick, and she found Benny and Miss Amelia in bed together. I guess Miss Amelia got dressed and left, and then Benny and Miss Dakota had a big fight. Miss Dakota left for California that night, and we never saw or heard from her again."

"So what happened between Benny and Amelia?" Ausitn asked, wantin to know as he got done peelin one potato and picked up another one.

"Three Sunday mornins later Miss Amelia was sittin by Benny in church, and she didn't have her engagement ring on anymore. Mr. Jeffery came to church with a new girl who was on him like flies on butter." Miss Shirely explained as she finished peelin the potato she had in her hand. "Miss Darlene was happy that Benny and Amelia were tryin things again, and She prayed that they would work out this time. In the summer of nineteen sixty-nine the two went up to New York state to go to the Woodstock concert like many other young people in the US. They told it was so much fun to be around like-minded people who just wanted live and love without war. We were the older generation and understood to a point, but we didn't under- stand why the younger generation needed to take at the drugs to feel happy."

"Oh wow! I would have loved to have been there with all the music, and just to see all the people at the event."

"Benjamin and Amelia made the trip back to Mississippi two months after the show, and they stopped in Memphis to attend a church that he had heard about from one of his friends. While they were at the church the preacher came up to Benjamin and told him that he would have his own ministry. The lord told him that he would touch many people's lives and lead them to the savoir Jesus. He would teach them that even though the road to get to Jesus may be long, short, or curvy it was all worth it for the lessons they had to learn along the way. The two of them got married in nineteen seventy, and Benjamin had started his own gospel group. Amelia was one of his backup singers, and the two loved travelin the country sharin the lord's word."

"Oh, wow!" Austin said, as he finished his last potato and put it down on the plate with the rest of them. "What was the name of the group?"

"Benjamin decided to name is group Southern Storytellers. Tragedy struck in nineteen seventy- four when the two were drivin to Baldwyn to eat at the local catfish house."

"What happened?" Austin asked, not seein that curve ball comin into the tellin of their lives.

"Benjamin was drivin when a car come from the on comin traffic and hit them head on. Amelia died Instantly, and Benjamin was rushed to the hospital. He had a broken leg and arm and many broken ribs. The sad part was

184

that Amelia's family had her funeral before he got out of the hospital, so he didn't even get to see her one last time before she was lowered into the ground. "

Austin couldn't say anything he just started cryin because the news of what happened to Amelia hit him hard. As he sat the knife down to get a paper towel to wipe his eyes Austin said, "Wow! How did he deal with the pain of that? What happened to him?"

"After Amelia died Benjamin couldn't function at all, and then he learned that she was three months pregnant with their child." Miss Shirley said, as tears streamed down her face. "Benjamin started drinkin more heavily and turned to the hard drugs so he didn't have to feel anything. He would disappear for weeks at a time, and we had no idea where he was at. By the late summer of nineteen seventy-nine, Benjamin had become the shell of the man he used to be. As the summer turned into autumn Benjamin started goin to church again, and we hoped that he would find himself once again.

Then one Sunday mornin at church Benjamin met a woman by the name of Molly Higgins. She was a tall and beautiful woman with long blonde hair and sparklin green eyes."

"Oh, wow!" Austin said, as he thought about Jaelyn as she described her.

"Miss Molly was Mr. Jeffery's baby sister, and he was very protective of her." Mrs. Shirley explained, as she and Austin started cuttin up the potatoes that were on the plate. "Mr. Jeffery didn't like it when Benjamin started talkin to his sister because he thought Benny was bad news. Mr. Jeffery was still upset that Amelia dumped him to go back out with Benjamin. It didn't matter though Miss Molly was a grown woman, and she let her brother know that she could date anybody she wanted to."

"So, what happened?"

"Benjamin and Molly fell in love with each other very quickly, and Molly moved in with Benjamin after only three weeks of datin. She took such great care of Benny, and he seemed to be doin really good. Still, there were nights when the memories of the war would come back to haunt him, and the night terrors of what happened to Amelia and their little baby."

186

"So, he never got over losin Amelia?"

"He never did get over losin her because she was the love of his life, and he would tell you fhat right in front of Miss Molly."

"Kind of somethin I do when it comes to my relationship with Jaelyn." Austin said, shakin his head. "I've never thought about how it affects her. I'm sure she thinks that she has no real chance with me since I can't get over Jessica."

"Yes child, she probably does."

"I need to be more respectful to her, and try to start livin in the moments I have with her instead of what could have been."

"That's a good idea." Mrs. Shirley said, with a big smile. She was happy that Austin was gettin somethin out of the story, and that Benjamin was helpin him in his own way. "Benjamin and Miss Molly got engaged in the summer of nineteen eighty and planned to get married in September of that year. They spent the rest of the summer plannin it with help from both of their parents. It was goin to be a good day because somethin new was beginnin, and there were goin to be great things happenin in both of their lives."

187

"Somethin happened didn't it?" Austin said, as he put the potatoes in the water on the stove.

"Yes, it did." Mrs. Shirley said, as she wiped tears from her eyes. "A week before the weddin that September a few of Benjamin's army buddies had come to visit him. It was all good and fine until there was no movement at Benjamin's house for a few days, so the cops were called and they broke the door down to get into the house to check on Benjamin. They found him lyin on the bed with a syringe in his arm, and a picture of him and Amelia lyin next to him."

"Oh, my god!"

"Whether it was the thought of movin forward with his life with Miss Molly, or his army buddies brought up a thing from the war that put him over the edge we'll never know."

"What happened to Molly?"

"It took her a while, but she moved on and married a real estate agent in Tupelo, but in nineteen eighty-two she was hit by a drunk driver and was killed instantly."

"Oh, wow! I didn't expect that to happen to her. What happened to Reva? I forgot to ask about her."

"After high school she made her way up to New York City, and went to Julliard for dance. She landed a few shows after graduation, but it was nothin spectacular. She married a guy named Eddie Princeton, and the two had a son name Evan Roccha."

"Why does Evan have his mother's last name?"

"Because she didn't want him to be ashamed of his father because he was a very bad druggy and left her and Evan for someone else. Reva have a very bad time after movin home, and not long after Benjmain passed away Reva overdosed on drugs leavin her parents to raise her son."

"Wow! That's just crazy the way life worked out." Austin said, with sadness in his eyes as he thought about what he had just heard.

The next seven days seemed to fly by very quickly, and to Eloise's dismay Austin seemed to spend more time with Jessica than he did with her. Eloise didn't understand how that little girl could capture Austin's attention so quickly. Austin also spent time learnin about Benjamin as Mrs. and Mr.

Schlatter told him stories of their son, and Ms. Shirley also told him a few more stories about Benjamin and the trouble he would get in to. Austin got up Sunday mornin bright and early so that Mrs. Shirley could tell him a few more stories about Benjamin before he left for Illinois. The Schlatter's told him to take a box of things of Benjamin's so that he could learn more about him because they didn't have the stories that Benjamin could tell him in his writins and other things. Austin went into Benjamin's house and got a box of notebooks that he had found in the closest to read when he got back home to Georgetown. Austin showed up to our church just as Eloise, Lee , Ann, Christine, and Beverly had started singin the mornin hymns. He had found a seat in the back, and just looked around the church as the Rev. Schlatter made his way to the podium and said, "God is our refiner and purifier. He purifies us like silver or gold as he takes the bad things that are in us and burns it out with his fire. And if it should come back to tempt us again we will not give into it. The lord wants us to shine like gold and be a light in this dark world."

"Amen." The congregation yelled.

"In Malachi three; two and three it says that but who can endure the day of his comin, and who can stand when he appears? For he is like a refiner's fire and like fuller's soap. He will sit as a refiner and purifier of silver, and they will bring offerins in righteousness to the lord. In Psalms fifty one; seven it says that god needs to purify us with hyssop, so that we can be white as snow."

"Oh, come on now." An elderly man yelled, from the back row.

"If we want to do any good in this world we first have to make ourselves clean, and because if we stay unclean we won't have the power to make a difference in anyone's life because we are just like them. We have purify ourselves and make ourselves refined just like Daniel twelve; ten says. our testimony won't save any lives if we still go back and do the same things we did yesterday. We are set apart from the other right now because we have to be the light that guides them to the truth. That Jesus is the only way to get to heaven, and yes there are many ways to get to him, but we only have one God who knows each and every one of us. "

"Preach it." A middle-aged woman said, with a big smile on her face.

"Jesus went to the cross and shed his blood for all of us not just the few who have made him our lord and savior. We have to go outside of these church walls and talk about him to a lost and dyin world because we're not helpin anyone if we stay in here and preach to choir. People who are

191

already saved and know the truth." Rev. Schlatter said, as he wiped his
forehead off with a handkerchief as sweat run down his face. "Too many
of us like to sit on our high horse and judge someone we don't know,
an do not want to know because their journey is different than ours. We
can't even find our purpose until we start to listen to what the lord has to tell
tell us, and can we do it in this world that is always full of noise?"

"No!" many from the congregation yelled.

"We have to be determined to want to uncover just why God sent us to
the earth at this time. We also have to be determined to find out what it is
exactly you and I are here to do on the earth to help our fellow men with
their journey. Like or not what we do affects others around the world, and it
can be good, bad, or indifferent. So, I ask you right now are you willin to dig
deeper and ask the lord why am I here? What is it you want me to do
while I'm here? How can helpin others help me in my journey? "

"Bring it home." The elderly man from the back yelled.

"To find those answers we have to draw closer to God just like it says
in James four eight God will start to draw nearer to us if we do that. Those

storm clouds will go away, and sunshine will lighten your path to where you need to go. This isn't just a one-time thing you have to do it every day, and believe that the lord will guide your steps to where your final destination is. Always look to the word because it is a light unto your path it will also help guide you to the people you will meet and the lives you'll change with god's help. Remember, to always give thanks to him because he is the reason you are here and humble yourself before him because without him you are nothin. If God does a work through you don't boast about it because you are bringin the light to yourself and what you did not what he did. Do it without wantin to have others praise because it will lead you down a path of destruction. Lord, before we leave here today I ask that those words come back to their remembrance. Let them realize that into order to be a light in darkness the darkness has to be burned out of them. I ask this in Jesus name, amen." Rev, Schlatter said, as he looked out on his congregation.

As the silence was broken with chatter Austin made his way around the sanctuary tellin people goodbye, and that he would see them soon. When he got to Jessica and her family it was kind of sad because she didn't want him to leave, but Austin told her that he would be sendin letters soon to let

her know what he was up to the two hugged and Jessica didn't want to

let go of Austin's neck, and it took Mr. Roccha pullin her away from him to

get Austin free. When Austin walked out of the church Jessica was cryin,

and we all realized how close the two had gotten over the summer since he

he spent so much time over at the Roccha's house. We could all see that

Eloise was upset that he was spendin more time sayin goodbye to Jessica

than he did her, and it made me wonder if she broke up with me last

summer because she wanted to go out with Austin.

Chapter Three

Our Senior Year

Austin made the long trip back to Illinois and he got home around eleven o' clock that Sunday evenin. Austin called Eloise to let her know that he had made it home safely, and that the two would talk more soon. His siblins were glad to see him home the next day when he finally got out of bed at three o' clock the next afternoon. They asked him all about his trip and did he get into any into any trouble while he was down there. His parents soon started askin him twenty questions because they wanted to know exactly what he did while he was away those three weeks. Austin gave them the short version and told them it was an interestin trip. He also told them it was one that he wouldn't forget anytime soon because of the history he had learned while he was down there. Austin had skimmed through a few things that he brought home from Benjamin's house, but he hadn't looked at it good enough to really understand Benjamin's state of mind when he wrote it.

Austin had also took time to look at the pictures that had been taken over the summer, and copies had been made for him to have. The one picture he put in a picture frame on the nightstand was a picture of him and little Jessica Roccha. The two were sittin in a booth together eatin catfish when Jessica's mother snapped a photo of them. Austin's brother Brandon looked at the picture a few times, but couldn't understand why his brother would put it in a frame and sit in on the nightstand.

Down here in Mississippi, Eloise and the girls had gone clothes shoppin for the first day of school. I was still workin hard at the diner makin sure I saved all my money to get the car I really wanted to drive instead of the hand me down car I got from parents. I was ready to get my last year of high school over with, but I had no idea what I wanted to do after I got out of high school. I was content with washin dishes for the rest of my life, but I know my parents wanted me to aim higher and do somethin that would help someone else.

Durin a hot muggy stretch of Mississippi weather Eloise and the rest of the girls came to the diner for supper. Most of the ladies that worked at the diner wished that they had as much energy as those young girls had. They watched them and wondered what could be makin them laugh so much, so they listened in close to hear what they were talkin about..

"So have you talked to Austin since he went home?" Beverly asked, as she took a drink of her milkshake.

"Yes, he called me when he got home to tell me he made it." Eloise replied, as she took a bite of a french fry.

"So, what happened between the two of you?" Lee Ann asked, as she took a bite of her french fry.

"He and I made out a few times over the summer." Eloise replied, crackin a big grin.

"You did?" Christine asked, shocked to hear that from Eloise.

"Yes, we did."

"Wait? So the two of you didn't go all the way?" Beverly said, caught off guard by her answer.

"That's right." Eloise explained, as she looked at all of them. "But I was really hopin that we would."

"So are you two datin?" Lee Ann asked, with a very serious look on her face.

"No, we're not datin."

"So what are the two of you?" Christine asked, tryin to understand the situation.

"We're friends, but I'm hopin that we'll become more."

"I wouldn't hold my breath Austin Reid is a cute guy and can have any girl he wants."

"I know that. I'm just hopin that I'm the girl that he wants"

"Well, after we all graduate from college you'll have all the time in the world to become more than friends with him since he is goin to be in our band." Beverly said, with a smile.

"Cousin, you know that she has to wait four more years before she can chase after him." Christine said, laughin as she took a drink of her pop. "The band isn't officially goin to start performin around the country until we all graduate from college."

"If I were you, Eloise. I would chase him now, and that way you know that you'll always be in his life until you want to take it to the next level."

"That's not a bad idea." Eloise replied, as she thought about Beverly's idea.

"Yes, but you can't chase after him too much otherwise he'll get tired of you chasin him."

"You have to make him know that you're interested but then pull away and go out with another guy." Lee Ann said, as she got ready to take a bite of her sandwich.

"Lee Ann's right." Beverly said, with a big smile. "You need to find a guy around here you can hang out with, but you have no intention of fallin for."

"And who would that be?" Christine said, as she rolled her eyes. "What guy is dorky enough that you wouldn't fall in love with him?"

"How about Waldo Wallace?"

"That guy is a nerd." Eloise replied, with a funny look on her face. "Why would I go out with that guy."

"Because he is harmless." Beverly said, crackin a big smile. "And it will make Austin Reid jealous because you are datin someone else."

199

"I'll have to think about it."

"Well, it would make Austin want you more since he can't have you once you are datin Waldo." Lee Ann said, with a big smile and a laugh.

"Is Austin Reid worth havin?" Christine asked, crackin a big grin as she took a bite of chocolate.

Eloise just looked at them for a few minutes knowin that they had a point. If she seemed to be taken maybe that would make Austin Reid want her more, but what if it backfired and her plan didn't work at all. After takin a deep breath she said, "I'm goin to think about it because I'm still not sure I can do it."

On Sunday mornin in Illinois it was church as usual for Austin and his family, and when Austin walked into the church Jaelyn ran over and hugged him so happy to see him. The two made their way into the sanctuary where they could talk before the church service started. Reese, Hope, Peyton, Jaedyn, and a few other girls wondered why Austin hadn't called Jaelyn to tell her that he was home. They wondered what secrets from what happened the last three weeks was he hidin from Jaelyn. Everyone else soon made their way into the sanctuary, and the choir members took their spot in the loft waitin to sing the mornin hymns. After the choir sung the mornin hymns the preacher walked up to the podium and said, "Please turn to Matthew 25:34. When you get it say amen."

A few minutes later people across the congregation started to say amen, and once a sufficient amount of people said it the preacher said, "In this parable a man was goin on a journey and entrusted his property to his servants. He gave one servant five talents, another he gave two talents to another, and he gave the last servant one talent. The one that received five talents went and made five talents more, and the one he gave two talents to made two more talents, but the one he gave one talent to went and buried in the ground. So, what do you think happened when it was time to settle up the accounts?"

"Oh, preach it!" An older grey-haired gentleman in the back of the church yelled.

"When the man came back to settle the accounts the first servant came to him and told him that he had made five more talents. The man told him well done my good and faithful servant. You have been faithful over little, and he would set him up with much more. The servant he gave two talents came to him and told him that he had made two more talents. The man explained that he would do the same for him as he will do for the first one."

"Preach it! Preacher!" A middle-aged older woman yelled, from the middle of the room.

"The servant who was given the one talent came to the man and told him that he did not like to reap where he didn't sow and gather where he had scattered seed. The servant told the man that he was afraid and went and hid the talent in the ground. The servant handed the man the talent and the man said that the servant was wicked and slothful. The servant knew where he reaped where he didn't sow and gathered where he hadn't scattered seed. He told the servant he should have went to the banker because the man expected interest for the talent. "

"Keep goin!" An older gentleman from the back row yelled.

"Just like those talents the master gave his servants we all have talents within us." The preacher explained, as he looked up at the congregation. "We all have talents to do certain things and when we do those things more talents that are within us come to the surface. We find out we can do much more than we thought we could. Everything we have to succeed in life is within us we just have to reach down deep to find what were called on earth to do. Don't run away from what God has called you to do because you end up just like Jonah. You'll end up causin bad things to happen to other people because you are around, and God is tryin to get your attention. "

"Preach it." An elderly woman in the middle of the church said, very happily.

"You'll be thrown off that boat because you will realize that you're the reason why the boat is sinkin, and the group of people you're around will want you off that boat because the boat won't sink if you aren't on it. then you'll be eaten up by a whale and in his belly for days."

"Oh yea!" The older grey-haired gentleman from the back row yelled.

"When you realize you need to do what God has called you to do that whale will throw you up just like he did Jonah, and you will go to Nineveh to tell the people they need to repent and turn back to God." The preacher said, very seriously as he looked at his congregation.

An hour later after talkin about Jonah and how Jesus went for the cross for everyone one of us the preacher finally finished his sermon. The preacher was so energetic when preachin it that Austin paid very close attention to it because he felt like the lord was talkin to him. Austin realized that this was the second time that God had talked to him about doin what he wanted him to do, and he realized that the lord had put his dreams in his heart for a reason. Austin knew that he was goin to chase after his dreams, and help as many people as he could along the way.

Later that afternoon Austin had laid down to take a nap, and after about thirty minutes Austin was sound asleep and off in dreamland where he was settin on the porch swing swingin when someone familiar walked up onto the porch and said, "Sunshine, is everything all right?"

"Yes, Satnin. I'm just wonderin how I can chase my dreams and not hurt Jaelyn?" Austin replied, as he looked up and over at her with a very serious look on his face.

"You need to chase your dreams because people in this world need you.." Jessica said, as she set down beside him on the swing.

"Why do they need me?"

"To help and inspire them to chase after their own dreams."

"What about Jaelyn?"

"Jaelyn doesn't matter because you have to do what you're called to do."

"Really?" Austin asked, as he looked into her blue eyes.

"Yes." Jessica replied. "Those people that God chose for you to inspire will chase after their dreams that will inspire the next generation, and the cycle keeps goin around."

"What if Jaelyn wants me to not to do it?"

"Then those people won't be inspired to chase after their dreams, and go down a road that will lead them to destruction."

"I didn't realize the domino effect that it would have on other people's lives."

"Not chasin after your dreams will affect other's lives, and it will affect your life as well."

"How?"

"You may go down a destructive road that will lead you to a fate you never thought you would be at."

"How do you know all this?"

"I have my sources." Jessica replied, crackin a little a grin. "Just promise me that you will chase after your dreams."

205

"I will." Austin said, as he put his arms around her and pulled her closer to him.

Jessica put her head on his shoulder smellin his familiar cologne, and enjoyed gettin that moment in his arms before she woke up from her nap down in Mississippi. Jessica wished she could grow up faster and be with him. Jessica knew that both she and Austin had lessons to learn before they could be together again.

A few days later Austin had gone through some of the recent pictures that had been taken of him along with some pictures from years past that the family had doubles made. He knew that she would get a kick out of him seein him playin on the Georgetown Fair stage, but he didn't know how well she would like seein a picture of him with Jaelyn on the stage. Austin decided to send the picture anyway just so that she would have them. He then chose the best pictures of him in his football uniform and him playin on the football field makin plays. He also decided to send a few pictures of Austin with his family durin the holidays as they played tricks on each other durin Thanksgivin and Christmas. After he had picked all the pictures out, he set down on his bed and started to write his first letter to Jessica.

He wrote her name and then leaned up against the headboard of the bed. As he put a book under his notebook, Austin thought about what he should write and how he should word it. He knew that her parents would be readin the letter to her so he wouldn't have to word it where she could read it.
The letter read;

Dear Jessica,

I hope this letter finds you well, and that you are enjoyin the rest of your summer. I just got done goin through the pictures that have been taken of me over the last few years, and I picked the ones that you would like. I know that in a few there will probably be a person that you don't want to see, but I'm gettin water throwed on me so I figured you'd think it was funny. I know that you'll probably be gettin a picture album to put them in, and I will send more later as they are taken of me. I can't wait to hear from you.

Your friend

Austin Reid

The next mornin Austin took the big envelope to the post office to mail it, and the woman at the counter looked at him a little funny once she read the name on the envelope. After he did that it was time to go to football practice, and most of his day was filled with runnin laps and runnun plays with his fellow teammates. By the time practice was over Austin was beat and he just wanted to go home and go to bed, but instead he went home and took a shower because his family was havin people over for a party that evenin. After he got out of the shower, he set on the bed and picked up the picture of him and Jaelyn from the nightstand. He wondered if she would ever understand his need to chase after his dreams. He was leanin up against the headboard lyin on the bed in nothin but his boxer shorts when the bedroom door opened and a familiar face walked in and said, "Hey, stranger."

"Hi, sweetness." Austin said, as he looked up from the picture smilin at her.

As she shut the door Jaelyn locked it because she didn't want anyone walkin in on them, and as she walked over to the bed she cracked a grin and said, "Not often that I get to see you in your boxer shorts, Mr. Reid. "

"Your mother would have a cow if she walked in on us."

"I know, but she won't walk in on us."

"Oh, really?" Austin said, as he laid the picture down on the bed.

"I locked the door.." Jaelyn said, as she leaned over and gave Austin a kiss. "Nobody will be walkin in on us."

"You want to get us both in trouble, don't you?"

"I would like to make a little trouble with you."

"I would love to make a little trouble with you.." Austin said, as he put his arms around her and pulled her closer to him.

Jaelyn just laughed as she put her arms around his neck and passionately kissed him. It wasn't long before the two were lyin on the bed makin out lost in each other's eyes not worryin about what was goin on outside of Austin's bedroom door. Jaelyn was happy that she finally had all of Austin's attention after him bein gone for those three weeks.

Two hours later Austin and Jaelyn still hadn't come down from his bedroom, and Jaelyn's mother was gettin really nervous. She didn't like it when Austin and Jaelyn were alone together for long periods of time because she assumed that Austin would talk her daughter into somethin that she shouldn't.

Just before seven o' clock Mrs. Somerled made her way through the house, and upstairs outside of Austin's room. She knocked on the door and said, "Austin, Jaelyn, what are you two doin in that room?"

"We're just talkin, Mom." Jaelyn replied, as she looked over at Austin with a big smile.

"Why is the door locked?"

"We didn't want Reese, Peyton, or any of the other girls to come in and bother us."

"Well, I think it's time that two of you join the party."

"Ok, Mrs. Somerled." Austin replied, enterin the conversation. "We'll be down in a few minutes."

"If you're not down by the pool in ten minutes." Mrs. Somerled said, with a very stern voice. "I will have your father come up here and make the two of you get out of this room."

"Yes, ma'am."

Mrs. Somerled walked away from the door, and looked back at the door because she got the sense that somethin more was goin on in Austin's room than what they were sayin. After makin her way back through the house and back outside to the party was goin on, she noticed that Lane was lookin over at her husband,. Mrs. Somerled thought for a brief moment that Lane was checkin her husband out. When Mrs. Somerled looked again Lane was talkin to someone and not payin attention to her husband anymore.

Back upstairs in Austin's room Austin kissed Jaelyn on the lips and as he pulled his lips away said, "I can't believe that we had sex with all those people downstairs."

"I know." Jaelyn said, as she looked into his ice blue eyes. "But I'm so happy that we did because I missed you so much while you were gone."

"Sweetness, I love you."

"I love you, cupcake." Jaelyn said, as she leaned up and passionately kissed him on the lips.

In that moment, Austin and Jaelyn forgot about the party that was goin on outside that they needed to attend. The two were so focused on each other that they didn't want to spend time with anyone that afternoon. Just as the two were startin to make love to each other again, there was a loud bang on the door and Austin's father tellin them that they better get down to the party. Otherwise, he was goin to get the key to the door and unlock it to find out what they were doin.

As much as Austin and Jaelyn hated it, they got dressed and joined the party that was goin on downstairs. All their friends were wonderin what the two of them were up to in his room all that time together alone. Even though Reese knew that Austin and Jaelyn were datin she still flirted with Austin right in front of Jaelyn. After what had happened upstairs Jaelyn didn't worry about Reese tryin to steal Austin away from her. A few hours later Reese watchin Austin and Jaelyn and she could see that somethin had changed between them because they were more expressive about showin their affection to each other in public.

A few days later Jaelyn was sittin in her room just lookin at a picture of her and Austin, thinkin about what had happened between the two of them. She felt disappointed in herself because she promised her mother when she became a teenager that she would wait until marriage to do that. She knew that her mother would be very disappointed in her because her mother held both her and Jaedyn to high standards. Jaelyn was wipin tears from her eyes when her sister Jaedyn walked into the doorway and asked, "Everything all right, sis? Do you want to talk?"

"Yes, and I would love to talk." Jaelyn replied, as she looked up at her sister. "But you have to close the door so mom doesn't hear us.'

As she walked into the room and shut the door Jaedyn asked, "What have you done, Jaelyn?

"I did somethin so wonderful, but I know that mom would ground me if she found out."

As Jaedyn sat on the bed she did notice that her sister looked different than she did just a few days before so she asked, "What did you do?"

"I had sex with Austin." Jaelyn replied, with the biggest smile on her face so happy.

"You did? When?"

"At the pool party Austin's parents had."

"Is that why the two of you were up in his room all that time." Jaedyn asked, crackin a huge grin.

"Yes."

"So how was he? And how was it?"

 "Austin was so gentle with me, and he kept askin me if I wanted to S top but I told him no. It did hurt but it was good."

"Was it his first time too?" Jaedyn asked, just bein nosy.

"No." Jaelyn replied, with sadness in her eyes.

"Who was his first? Was it Reese or Hope?"

"His first was Rosanna Aydelotte when she was here that Thanksgivin."

"No way! He told you that?"

"Yes, I asked him about it before he left this summer."

 "I can't believe it my little sister has become a woman before her sopho-more year of high school."

 "You're not goin to tell anyone are you?" Jaelyn asked, wonderin if her sister would hold it over her until they both were out of high school.

"I'm not goin to tell anybody." Jaedyn replied, with a big smile. "Unless I need a favor…"

Mrs. Somerled was walkin down the hallway with a load of dirty clothes in a basket when she noticed that Jaelyn's bedroom door was closed. She looked into Jaedyn's room and found that she wasn't in her room, so she wondered what the girls might be up to with Jaelyn's bedroom door closed. Mrs. Somerled knocked on the door and asked, "Girls, is everything all right?"

"Yes, mom, we're just talkin." Jaelyn yelled, loud enough where her mother could hear her.

"Why is the door locked?"

"Jaedyn must have locked accidentally when she came into my room."

"I'll unlock it, mom." Jaedyn said, as she walked to the door and unlocked it.

As she walked back and set on the bed Mrs. Somerled opened the door and said, "What are you two talkin about that the door has to be locked?"

"We were talkin about Austin and wonderin what he did for the three weeks he was out of town." Jaelyn explained lyin through her teeth.

"Are you worried you that he was with someone while he is gone?"

"Yes, mother I am."

"If he was then he's not the man for you." Mrs. Somerled said, as she set on the bed with her daughters.

"I know, but I love him." Jaelyn said, startin to wonder if he was with someone while he was gone over the summer.

Down here in Saltillo Austin's letter finally arrived at the Roccha farm, and Jessica was so happy that she would get to look at the pictures he had sent her. She was very impressed with the pictures of Austin in his football uniform and the pictures of him makin plays durin a game. As she picked up one of the pictures of Austin on stage with Jaelyn Jessica said, "I don't like that girl."

"Why?" Mrs. Roccha asked, with a laugh as she looked at her daughter.

"She's datin the boy I'm goin to marry one day." Jessica said, as she looked up at her mother with a very serious face.

"How do you know that you are goin to marry Austin Reid?"

"I just know."

"Tell me how you know, Jessi." Mrs. Roccha said, as she took the picture from Jessica's hand and looked at it.

"We were together in my last life and dreamed of bein married since we were young kids. I know that he will pick me over her when I get old enough."

"What if he marries that girl before he marries you?"

"I'm goin to steal him away from her." Jessica said, with a big smile on her face as she took a bite of her cookie.

"Really? You are?"

"Yes, mama, I am."

"And you think he'll leave her for you?"

"He will, mama. He loves me more than he will ever love that girl." Jessica said, before she took a drink of milk out of her glass.

"You sure are sure of yourself, Jesscia." Mrs. Roccha said, with a big smile and laugh.

"I know Austin Reid better than anyone else, and I know that he will pick me over that girl any day once I'm old enough."

"So, that's what me and your father have to look forward to. You bein with a man a lot older than you."

"Yes, mama." Jessica said, with a big smile on her face that puzzled her mother.

A week later it was time for the Georgetown Fair, and all the kids in town were so excited to go It was a week filled with corn dogs, fair rides, grandstand events, other fried fair foods, but the for the young kids in town it could be their first experience at a fair. They get to try cotton candy for the first time and find out that they really like it. The first night of the fair Austin and Jaelyn took his younger siblins to hang out with their friends. Austin and Jaelyn rode the rides too along with playin the fair games, and it wasn't a surprise that there were people watchin them. It was like they were mad because he had moved on with his life. Tuesday night was really a competition because Austin was in the talent show and so were the Somerled sisters. Austin chose to sing the song "My Eyes Adored You" by Frankie Valli. It was a surprise to Jaelyn because she thought that he was goin to sing another Elvis song like he always had, and she knew that he was singin the song for Jessica and not for her. Jaedyn

thought about it, and started to think that he was singin the song
to Jaelyn because she knew that Austin was still thinkin about leavin town
after graduatin from high school. Jaedyn told Jaelyn that she thought Austin
was singin the song to her because he was still strugglin with the decision to
leave town or not. Jaelyn wasn't convinced because durin the time he was
in fifth and six grade he was with Jessica. After Austin was done singin it
was the Somerled sisters turn, and they sang the song "(They Long To
Be) Close to You." Austin knew that Jaelyn was singin the song about
him because she had experienced many girls wantin to be close to him.
Once again Robbie Wallison won the talent show, and it went straight
to head.

  After the talent show was over Austin and Jaelyn had gotten somethin
to eat at one of the many food vendors and had set down in the food buildin
to eat it. Austin had just taken a bite of his curly fries when a group of girls
walked up. A tall bean pole teenage girl with shoulder length blonde
haired and bright brown eyes asked, "Austin, can we get your autograph
and a picture?"

  After Austin finished chewin his curly fry Austin flashed his boyish smile
as he wiped his hands and said, "Of course, you can."

Austin got up and the girls started takin turns gettin their picture taken with him, and then he started to sign the pieces of paper they had in their hands. The entire time Jaelyn just watchin him enjoyin every minute gettin the attention from girls he didn't know. In that moment, she remembered the look on Jessica's face when girls that Austin didn't know walked up and started talkin to him. Jaelyn was only in the third grade, but she remembered that Jessica didn't want to share him with the new fans he got every time he performed at the talent show. Jaelyn did notice that the girls were stuffin somethin into his pants pockets, and she was goin to find out what they were later.

That night after the fair was over Austin drove Jaelyn home and walked her onto the front porch. The two set on the front porch swing and felt the cool August wind blow.Jaelyn then started diggin into Austin's pockets, and as he watched her do it Austin laughed and asked, "Sweetness, what are you doin?"

"I want to see what those girls put in your pockets." Jaelyn replied, as she pulled out a handful of small pieces of paper.

"It's probably nothin."

"I think it is somethin, and I'm goin to find out what it is."

"You are silly, Jaelyn." Austin said, as he picked up one of the pieces of paper that had fallen on his leg.

As she opened up a few of the pieces of paper, Jaelyn saw the girl's names and their phone number. As she folded the paper back up she looked at Austin and said, "I told you.. It is their name and phone numbers wantin you to call to them."

"You know I wouldn't do that."

"Do I? You seemed to be havin a lot of fun takin pictures with them. Would you call Mallory and hang out with her?"

As he folded the piece of paper he had, and handed it to Jaelyn he replied, "Sweetness, they are just fans of mine, but you are the fan I want to be with."

"Now, you are just sweet talkin me." Jaelyn said, as she threw the paper down on the porch and looked into Austin's ice blue eyes.

"Why would I do that?"

Jaelyn gave him a kiss on the lips and as she pulled back she asked, "Why did you sing that song tonight? Who was it about?"

"I sang that song because I felt it was the right song to sing." Austin said, as he stretched out his arm across the back of the swing. "And I sang it about us. Because I want to go to New York and chase after my dreams, but the hold you have on me that I can't explain makin me want to stay here with you."

"So it wasn't about Jessica?"

"Why would you think the song is about Jessica?"

"You were in fifth grade and with her, so it made me wonder."

"No, the song was not about her." Austin explained, as he leaned over and kissed her on the lips.

"Will you ever take the ring she gave you off your finger?" Jaelyn said, as she looked into his ice blue eyes already seein the answer.

"I don't know.. I might one of these days, but right now I'm goin to keep wearin it."

"Ok."

"Why would you ask me that question?"

"I was just curious." Jaelyn explained, as she put her arms around his neck and passionately kissed him on the lips.

Just as the moment started to get intense the front porch light went off and turned back on about five times. Jaelyn knew that it was time for Austin to go, but she wished he could stay a little bit longer. As Austin walked her to the front door and gave her a good night kiss he said, "Sweet dreams, sweetness."

Fair week went way too fast for everyone because the followin Monday Austin, Harley, Sophia, and Brandon started school in The Georgetown Ridge Farm school district. For the four of them it was just the same old borin day with new teachers to teach them. Lane started her first year of community college at the junior college in Danville, Illinois at DACC, Lane was a little stressed when she realized that a handful of her classmates were also goin to DACC, so every day she still felt that the dark cloud of high school followin her. Just like in high school though, she kept a notebook with her and she wrote durin class on Rodeo Dreams. It was in about the fourth rewrite and she would take characters out and put new ones in, but the story didn't change that much. Toward the end of August school was in full swing, and everyone was gettin into their normal routines. Lane was findin that gettin up and bein at an eight o' clock class wasn't the most easy thing to do on her own because she had already missed about four of them.

Austin, on the other hand, was enjoyin his senior year because he was a big man on campus along with all of the other senior teenage boys that played football that season. A lot of the teenage girls in the high school were jealous of Jaelyn because she was a sophomore, and datin the teen-age boy all of them really wanted to date. The girls wondered why Austin would date someone two years younger than him when there were girls in his own class that would like to go out with him. The teenage girls would watch Austin and Jaelyn as they walked through the halls holdin hand and talked to each other. Many of the freshmen girls wondered if they could steal him away from Jaelyn because they didn't believe the two were actually as in love as the two seemed to be. It wasn't long before the girls who talked to him at the fair dared Mallory to chase after Austin to see if she could still him away from Jaylen.

On Harley's birthday that year Harley, Lane, and their family got some bad news when their grandma Sutton got a call that her younger sister had passed away durin her sleep. It was a surprise to everyone in the family,

224

and the funeral was three days later in St. Louis. Lane took the passin of her great aunt really hard because she was always a cheerleader for Lane to chase after her dreams. She seemed to have more faith in Lane than Lane had in herself at the time. Lane went down with her mother to the ab funeral and it was a very hard day for her because she knew that no one would be cheerin for as loud as her great aunt did. Growin up she really had no one tell her that she could do anything that she put her mind to because it seemed that she was always disappointin those who were in her life to encourage her. After gettin back from the funeral Lane seemed to be in a tailspin, she started drinkin a lot more than she ever had before ready to throw her life away.

Then one cool September evenin she felt so bad thinkin no one in the world would miss her if she wasn't on the earth anymore, so Lane took about six pain pills. She thought that she wouldn't wake up in the mornin, but the sun shined brightly in her window the next mornin. After the third attempt to kill herself Lane got a revelation that changed her life forever. She realized that the devil was tryin to take her out because what her future held he didn't want her to accomplish because it would decrease his

kingdom by many. Lane wasn't sure exactly what her path was because she wanted to be a published author, but she also wanted to make
music As she sat there on the bed she started to wonder if her purpose
on earth was bigger than she thought it could be. Lane also started to
wonder if it had any connection to her past life because she didn't get to
finish somethin that she should have. Lane was hopin that when she
would go to sleep at night that the lord would show her more of her past
life, and reveal to her what her purpose on earth this time was.

A few days later she was settin on her bed as the sun shined through
her window Lane grabbed her notebook and a pencil and wrote a song in
about ten minutes. As she repeatedly read the words to herself she realized
that this was the piece of the puzzle she was missin because of all the
negative times she had in her life, but now she had to change her way of
thinkin every mornin as she faced a new day. Lane read these words;

In the mornin, I'm lyin there in bed

The devil puts negative thoughts in my head

Off the beaten path I was lead

By the angel that's spiritually dead

But on the word of God I fed

To start my day in a positive way

There are days my troubles aren't few

That's why Jesus I turned to you

When it seems I'm in a bind

I quote the scripture line by line

Cause I'm determined to stay

In a positive state of mind

When the mountains are tall

My backs up against the wall

To the world it's not secret at all

The devil wants me to stumble and fall

Tellin me the bible's words are null

So I won't hear the lord's call

There are days my troubles aren't few

That's why Jesus I turned to you

When it seems I'm in a bind

I quote the scripture line by line

Cause I'm determined to stay

In a positive state of mind

As everyone got used to the chilly September mornins, Austin would get up, get ready for school, and then go pick up Jaelyn to drive her to school. On a very chilly Thursday mornin Jaelyn rode with her sister Jaedyn because she had overslept and was runnin late. Austin decided to go ahead and go to the high school because he was already in town, so he parked his car and then went into the school. Austin had started to read one of Benjamin's notebooks, and Austin was surprised that it was a notebook that talked about is life with Molly Higgins. He was readin an entry in the notebook when a familiar tall bean pole young teenage girl with blonde shoulder length hair and brown eyed girl set across from him and said, "Hi, Austin."

Austin slowly looked up from the notebook and smiled as he said, "Hi, Mallory."

"What are you readin?"

Austin closed the notebook as he looked at her a little puzzled wonderin what it was that she wanted. As he cracked his boyish grin he asked, "What is it you want?"

"Where's your girlfriend?"

"She's runnin a little late this mornin, but she'll be here."

"Can I keep you company until she gets here?"

"Sure, I don't mind." Austin replied, kind of likin the attention he was gettin.

At seven fifty-five am Jaedyn and Jaelyn walked into the school, and the two waved at their dad who was across the room. Jaedyn then made her way over to where her friends were sittin when she noticed Austin talkin to the young girl. Jaedyn waved for her sister to come over to where she was, and Jaelyn who was talkin to her own friends wondered what could be so I important that her sister wanted her over by her.

Back at the table Austin and the young girl were laughin and havin a good time visitin with each other. After a few questions Mallory looked at Austin dead serious and asked, "So how come you didn't call me I gave you my number."

229

"Jaelyn saw you put the paper in my jean pocket and got it out before I could see it."

"Really, Reidsy?"

"Why would I lie to you.." Austin replied, crackin his boyish grin.

A few feet away Jaelyn was watchin with the rest of Jaedyn's friends what was goin on between Austin and Mallory because she couldn't hear what they were sayin. Jaelyn knew that she was goin to have to talk to Mallory durin volleyball practice because she thought that Mallory was one of her close friends because they had played basketball together in junior high. Jaelyn had told her years ago how much she wanted to be Austin's girlfriend, and now Mallory seemed to be tryin to steal him away from her.

"Here's my number." Mallory said, as the bell started to ring for the start of school. "Call me sometime and we can hang out together."

Austin took the number as he looked at her knowin that he was never goin to call her, but he wanted to be polite because that's how he was raised. As he cracked his boyish grin he replied, "Ok, maybe I'll call you."

Mallory walked away with a big smile on her face, and Austin looked around to see Jaelyn starin at him with a look on her face that he knew

230

that he was in trouble. As the two walked to class together Austin gave Jaelyn the piece of paper. He explained that he wasn't ever goin to call Mallory, and he was just bein polite because that's what his family had taught him to be.

That afternoon at volleyball practice Jaelyn and Mallory were on different teams, Jaelyn tried to drive the ball many times at Mallory. Mallory didn't know what was goin on so she did the same thing back to Jaelyn. There was sort of a fight only with the volleyball bein the weapon of choice. Late that afternoon after practice as the girls were changin clothes to leave Jaelyn looked at Mallory and said, "I heard a rumor that you were hittin on my boyfriend this morin?"

"Yes, I did." Mallory replied, with a little cockiness in her answer.

"Why?"

"Because I like him."

As Jaelyn walked closer to where Mallory was standin. "Do you really think that you stand any chance at all with my boyfriend."

"Yes, I do." Mallory said, as the two girls stood face to face with each other both determined to win the fight.

"I don't think you have a chance." Jaelyn said, startin to laugh as she looked at her.

"Why do you think that?"

"Because he's in love with me, and you're not his type."

"Really?" Mallory replied, with a giggle. "We both know that Jessica is the third person in your relationship, and you are just filliin the space that she left vacant."

"What did you say?" Jaelyn asked, upset waitin for her to say it again so she could throw the first punch.

"You heard what I said."

"Ok., that's enough." Jaedyn said, steppin in between the two of them knowin that her sister was gettin ready to throw a punch. "You two are friends and you're goin to let your friendship go over a guy that won't matter next week."

"I'm goin to say this one time and you better listen.." Jaelyn said, with a very serious look in her eyes as she pointed her finger at Mallory. "You stay away from my boyfriend, and if I hear that you are anywhere around him I'll beat you up."

"The question is can he stay away from me." Mallory said, with a big smile as she picked up her bookbag and made her way out of the locker room.

Jaedyn talked Jaelyn down so that she wouldn't chase after Mallory and beat her up. Jaedyn and Jaelyn talked the rest of the evenin about the chances of Austin really goin out with Mallory. They both knew that it was one billion to one that he would even give her a chance. Then Jaelyn talked to her sister about what Mallory said about her just bein a fill in for Jessica, and implin that Austin didn't really love her at all.

Homecomin week started on September twentieth, and everyone watched Austin because they wanted to see what he would do. To everyone's surprise he did show up to school that day, but he walked into the school alone because Jaelyn had ridden with her sister. She kept her distance from him that mornin because of the sad tellin look on his face, but by lunch time the two were settin together at the table talkin. That afternoon when Austin got home from school after football practice there was an envelope waitin on him. Austin walked up to his room, laid down on the bed, ripped open the envelope, started to look what was inside. He chuckled as he looked at the pictures that Mrs. Roccha had sent him of Jessica. Austin got out the scrapbook that he and Jessica started back in nineteen ninety and put the pictures in it. Then he unfolded the piece of paper that was

also in the envelope and started to read it,

The letter read;

Dear Austin,

I really liked the pictures you sent me a few weeks ago, and I really

liked the ones of you in your football uniform. I'm so glad you are playin

football like you wanted to when you were younger. I liked many of the

pictures you sent me of you on the Georgetown Fair stage singin, but I

didn't like the ones you sent with that girl. I know God sent her in your life to

help you move forward with your life, so that we could find each other again

but I'm jealous because she is gettin to share moments with you that I can't.

I know that I'm just a little girl, but I want to see you graduate from high school

because it means so much to me. I hope that you will let me and my family

come up and watch you walk across the stage, but if you don't I understand

because it would be two worlds clashin too soon. I hope that you write me

soon, and I can't wait to see more pictures of you.

Your Friend

Jessica

As homecomin week passed, Jaelyn saw a change in Austin because he

wasn't as sad as he had been like years before on the anniversary of Jessica's

234

kidnappin. Jaelyn found that a little confusin because he had always taken the anniversary week so hard in the past. Jaelyn decided to take it because she knew that the next year it could be a totally different story. When Austin wasn't travelin to watch Jaelyn play volleyball, Austin was at home divin into the notebooks of Benjamin Schlatter. He knew that it would help him when it came to his own life he was livin, so that he wouldn't make the mistakes that he had made in his life before. The homecomin game on Friday was very intense because both teams took the lead and then lost it. Austin made some very good plays, and helped the team win the game. After the game was over, Austin got changed and a huge group of people went out to Ryan Ackles house for a party. Ryan Ackles was a tall muscular man with a gorgeous smile and sky-blue eyes, and he was a senior classmate.

Teenage kids were everywhere on his parent's farm just outside of town, and many were around the bonfire. Of course, there were many little clicks at the party, and one click talkin about how they didn't like the other click for any reason. Austin was drinkin a beer sittin on a truck tailgate enjoyin the fire when Mallory walked up to him and said, "Hi, Austin."

"Hi, Mallory." Austin replied, crackin his boyish grin as he looked at her.

"Where's your girlfriend?"

"She's around here somewhere."

"Really?."

"Yes, really.." Austin said, with a big laugh as he finished the beer.

"How about you and I go for a walk?"

"I don't think that's a good idea."

"It's just a walk and I don't bite." Mallory said, with a big smile as she looked into his ice blue eyes.

"Go Austin." Rodney said, with a big smile as he looked at him. Rodney was also in senior class with Austin. He was a few inches taller than Austin, and was a very muscular man because he loved to work out. "I'm sure a walk is just what you need right now."

"I know better than to do this." Austin said, as he slid off the tailgate. "Ok, let's go for a walk."

Rodney just smiled thinkin he knew what was goin to happen between Austin and Mallory while the two of them were all alone in the dark. Jaelyn came lookin for Austin just a few minutes after Austin and Mallory disappeared in the dark, and Rodney told Jaelyn a lie about where Austin went. While she waited for Austin, Remy walked up and started talkin to her. Rodney watched as he saw Remy put his moves on put the moves on Jaelyn tryin to steal her from Austin.

Behind the faded red barn Austin and Mallory set on an old chevy backseat that was leanin up against it, and as they set down Austin asked, "What is it that you want from me, Mallory?"

"I want to give you the attention you're not gettin from Jaelyn." Mallory replied, with a big smile as she got off of the backseat and got on his lap.

"Why?"

"Because you deserved to be loved the right way."

"And you think that you are the girl who can do that?"

"I know I can" Mallory said, as she started kissin him on the neck.

"I don't think you can." Austin said, as he enjoyed the attention he was gettin from her. "And I'm in love with Jaelyn.."

"But can she love you the way you need to be loved?"

"She does love me the way I need to be loved."

"Then why are you back here with me." Mallory said, as she passionately kissed him on the lips.

"You told me we were goin for a walk." Austin replied, as he looked into her brown eyes.

"Reidsy, come on." Mallory said, as kissed him on the lips. "Jaelyn wants to be the perfect angel for mommy and daddy. You know that she would never do that until she's married."

"Really? And you know that how?"

"Everybody knows that she isn't goin to have sex until marriage because that's what she has told her friends for as long as I can remember."

"Ok, if you say so.." Austin said, as he looked at Mallory seein the determination in her eyes to be with him.

"I just want to be with you right now."

"No, that isn't goin to happen."

"Why not?"

"Because I don't want to be with you."

"Yes, you do." Mallory said, as she cracked a big grin as she kissed him "You would have left already if you didn't."

"How about I get up and leave right now."

"You're not leavin." Mallory said, still kissin him. "You want me just as much as I want you right now."

Austin didn't know it but Jaelyn had started lookin for him because he had been gone for so long. She made her way around the barn, and couldn't believe what she saw when she turned the corner. Five feet away she saw Austin makin out with Mallory. Jaelyn saw red as she marched over to where the two were sittin. As she watched Austin kissin Mallory Jaelyn yelled, "What the hell is goin on here?"

Austin stopped kissin Mallory, pushed her off of him, and said, "J, this isn't what it looks like."

"Of course, it's what it looks like." Mallory replied, with a big smile.

"You bitch! I warned you….." Jaelyn said, as she started after Mallory.

"Girl's!" Austin said, steppin in between them stoppin the fight.

"Austin, how could you?"

"I'm sorry, I didn't mean for it to happen."

"But it did happen.." Jaelyn asked, as she wiped tears from her eyes. "And you take it back.."

"I'm a little drunk, and one thing led to another." Austin explained, with an upset look on his face.

"That's no excuse. You willin kissed her over and over again."

"Can we go somewhere and talk about this?"

"I never want to see you again." Jaelyn said, as she wiped tears from her as she started to walk away from Austin.

"Sweetness, come on give me a chance to explain." Austin said, tryin to grab her arm as she walked away from him.

Saturday night was the homecomin dance at GRHS, and everyone was so excited to go and have a good time. Jaelyn decided to go with Remy because he didn't have a date, and she would make Austin jealous if he showed up to the dance. Two hours into the dance Jaelyn saw Mallory show up with a male classmate of hers, and Jaelyn realized that Austin wasn't comin to the dance at all. Jaelyn spent the rest of the dance hopin that would change his mind and show up to the dance just to have one dance with her.

Across town settin on his bed in his bedroom Austin had gotten out a different notebook to read because readin the other one didn't feel right since he and Jaelyn had broken up. As Austin read the entries in the journal, he realized just how in love Benjamin and Amelia were in high school. He and Amelia had all grown up together and found out they had been into each other since they were young, but no one really knew it because they kept it a secret from everyone that they knew.

241

Then came that dreadful day when he got drafted into the army, and their lives changed forever. He read the entries about goin to basic trainin and how hard the commandin officers tried to break their spirit so that they could mold them into the soldiers they wanted them to be. Then came the journal entries of bein shipped over to Vietnam and be a soldier in combat. Austin read many entries where he learned that Benjamin was havin a hard time with killin people even though they were the enemy because of what he had been taught in church. Then came the entry that really shocked Austin to the core because it was a journal entry that he wasn't expectin at all. The journal entry read;

Dear Lord,

I thank you for keepin me alive as I fight in this war to protect your people. Even though they may not know who they are I believe that every person on this earth comes from heaven. I'm learnin now that the world has many religions and beliefs, and I will admit that many of them I don't understand. I want to thank you for gettin me out of my little town, so that I can have more experiences and learn things that I don't understand. I didn't realize that there could be so many beliefs in one country from Shamanism,

Buddhism, Catholic, Christianity, and Islam. As I talk to the people I'm learnin so much about things that I was taught growin up in my Pentecostal church, and I'm realizin that we all want somethin to believe in. We need to believe that there is a high power lookin out for us twenty-four hours a day seven days a week. My grandfather would probably want to put me over his knee or take a switch from the backyard because I am takin in and learnin beliefs that he doesn't believe in. I'm sure that my grandpa wouldn't like it either because one person I met insisted that I have a shaman do a prote-ction ritual over me to keep me safe, and this was after I talked to her about you. Although I'm still not sure what your path is for me now that I'm in the army fightin for another country, I know that you will show me my path as I use your word as a lamp unto my feet to light my path as I walk home to you.

Your Son,

Benjamin

Austin turned the page, and he saw two letters folded up in between the next two pages. Bein curious Austin unfolded the letter and started to read it. The letter read;

Dear Amelia,

I hope this letter finds you well and that you are still makin straight

school. I miss you so much, and I can't wait to be home with you again.
I know that your sister is probably tellin you that I'm not bein faithful to you,
and I'm doin what all the other soldiers are doin but that's not true. I'm in love
with you, Milas, and bein thousands of miles away from you isn't goin to change
that. I'm just hopin that you will wait for me and not find anyone else while I'm
away. I'll talk to you soon.

Love,

Benjamin

Austin folded up the letter and set it back inside the journal, and he picked
up the second letter and unfolded it. As he skimmed over it as his eyes started
to fill up with tears, and as he read it the second time more tears streamed
down his face as the impact of the letter hit him like a ton of bricks. The
letter read;

Dear Benny,

I was so happy to hear from you and to know that you are ok. Yes, my
sister has been tellin me that I shouldn't trust you, and that you will break
my heart just like you did hers. I don't believe her though because I know
just how much you love me. My parents want me to break up with you, so
that's why I sent this letter to you. We can't see each other anymore you

have to move on with your life, and forget about the love we have for each other. Please don't write me any letters anymore, and I'm prayin that God will keep you safe while you are fightin in this war to keep the people of south Vietnam free from the north.

Love Always,

Amelia

Austin folded up the second letter and put it back into the notebook. As he shut the notebook, he started to think about Jessica and what life would have been like if she had broken up with him once she had gone into the air force. He knew that he would have been in just as a much of a tailspin as Benjamin was goin to go into. He started to wonder how he would have acted, and if he would have started datin Jaelyn once he got over the shock of Jessica breakin up with him. Then Austin wondered what it would be like if she had come back into town for a visit. How would she react to him datin someone else even though Jessica did still love him so much. After thinkin about it for quite a long time, Austin finally fell asleep and went off to dream-land. No surprise in his dream he had dreamed that Jessica had come home for a visit a few days into homecomin week. Austin did notice that she had come back home, and he saw her watchin him from the porch as he got into

245

his car to leave to go to school. The night of the football game Jessica was in the stands with her family, and she noticed that a young girl was wearin his football jersey. Jessica started to wonder if Austin had moved on with his life like she had told him to do, and not realizin that she wrote that letter to him when she goin through a rough time believin that she was capable of actually flyin a combat jet plane. After the game was over, Jaelyn made her way over to Austin givin him a kiss because she was so proud that the buffaloes had won the game. A few feet away Jessica watched in horror because her worst fear had come true.

The next mornin Jessica walked over to Austin's house and knocked on the door. His mother let her into the house, and she made her way up to his bedroom where he was soundly sleepin. She opened the bedroom door Jessica just watched him sleep for a few minutes before she walked over and sat on the bed next to him. She ran her fingers through his hair, and then she leaned down and kissed him on the lips. Austin turned over and said, "Good mornin, Jaelyn."

"It's not Jaelyn." Jessica said, a little upset that he would do that do her.

Austin opened his eyes and cracked his boyish smile as he looked up into her blue green eyes. Still a little shocked that she would be in his bedroom he said, "What are you doin here?"

"I wanted to talk to you."

"You said enough when you told me that you wanted to break up with me."

"Sunshine, listen." Jesscia said, as put her hand in his. "I wrote that letter when I was in a very bad place, and I should have never sent it because I didn't want to break up with you."

"Well, it's too late now." Austin said, as he set up against the headboard of the bed. "I've moved on with my life."

"I know, but I know you still love me."

"Of course, I love you. But you broke my heart when you broke up with me."

"I'm sorry, I hurt you, and I regret sendin that letter to you."

"Why didn't you send me another letter telln me that you didn't want to break up with me."

"I'm sorry, I wrote you another letter, but I didn't send it because I figured you wouldn't write me back."

"If you would have sent it." Austin said, as he leaned up and wiped the tears away. "I wouldn't be datin Jaelyn, and I would be datin you."

247

"Sunshine, I know that." Jessica said, as she took his hand. "Are you goin to break up with her, so we can be together."

"I will." Austin said, as he kissed her on the forehead. "But, you have to give me a little time."

Austin and Jessica spent the rest of the day together. Jessica told him about life in the air force, and how fun it was to fly fighter planes. She explained how fun it was to explore where she was stationed because she loved to learn history. Austin told her bornin it was in high school, but he did like that he playin football. He also told how he couldn't wait for the school year to get over so that he could join her where she was stationed.

In my own life. Eloise and the rest of us were gearin up for our homecomin, and by this time Eloise had started talkin to Waldo, and she found that the two had a few things in common. Although he was a short muscular heavy- set teenage boy, Waldo was on the football team and hung out with the popular crowd. Unlike many of the other football players on the team Waldo was a

248

straight A student and loved to read books about subjects he thought were interestin. By readin a little manual he got from the local gas station he learned to change the oil in his car. Eloise had forgotten about Austin since she seemed to be fallin in love with Waldo. Many people in the popular crowd couldn't believe that Eloise actually liked Waldo when all our lives she had called him a dweeb. It wasn't a shock when I heard that Eloise and her group of friends went to Memphis to find their dresses for home-comin, and they probably would go back to get dresses for prom too.

As September turned to October Austin and Jaelyn still weren't talkin. Mallory was doin her best to convince everyone that she and Austin were an item, but everyone saw that Austin would only talk to her a few minutes. Remy was doin his best to spend time with Jaelyn, but she would always come up with a reason not to. Remy would call her every evenin she was at home, and talk to her for an hour tryin to get her to really notice that he liked her.

Then as October turned to November Austin and Jaelyn started to talk to to each other with their eyes when they looked at each other. Both saw in each other's eyes the sadness that they weren't speakin to each other, but both were afraid to talk to each other.

249

Thanksgivin seem to come and go quickly, and while Jaelyn was at a basketball tournament Austin was at home and did more research on Benjamin as he read more of his journals along with lookin at the pictures he found. As he sat on his bed with just the light on the nightstand on since it was so light outside, he started to read in a journal that had a lot of wear. He got halfway through the book, and he found an entry that made him think about how he felt at the time. Granted the circumstances were different, but he felt the same way that Benjamin did at the time. He read the entry many times. The entry read;

Dear Lord,

It's a stormy rainy night as I sit here on this bed with a loaded gun in my hand, I'm tryin to decide whether I should take my life or not. I feel that I have nothin to live for because my life has fallen apart right before my eyes. You took Amelia away from me, and our little baby in that car wreck a few months ago. I'm so lost right now, and I know that I can't fulfill the purpose you have for me without her. She was the love of my life, and I don't want to live without her. I know I gave my life to you, and I lived my life every way but the way I should. I know that I have come close to tarnishin your name and mine at the same time.

Your Son,

Benjamin

In that moment of readin it memories seemed to come back to Austin. He could hear the thunder rollin outside along with the lightin strikin. The rain fallin down in buckets as he felt the cold metal of gun in his hand as he moved the gun up to his mouth, a loud clap of thunder rang out as I lightin flashed makin Benjamin fall to his knees on the floor. Benjamin repented of his sins and as he cried asked god to forgive him.

On Friday evenin Austin took the journal to Grandma Reid's when the family went over for dinner. Austin shared the entry with Lane because he thought that between the two of them they could make into a song to help people in the world strugglin with the same thing. Lane read the entry not once but at least ten times as she felt the pain that Benjamin felt as he wrote those words on the piece of paper. She realized that she had been in that same situation where she wanted to give up and just end her life. Austin told Lane all about Benjamin's life that he knew, and then Austin and Lane went upstairs with their guitars to try and come up with a song that they thought would help the world when the two got to record it. As they set on the cold floor in the bedroom on the right side of the hall the two played with chords as each one tried to find the right words. Two hours later the family heard the two of them strummin their guitars and singin the words they had written down in a notebook on a piece of paper. The two sang these words;

I was raised on the good book
Went to church every Sunday
Put on the righteous path
To the promise land

With yesterday's values gone
Listenin to the preacher preach
Jesus is comin back soon
And so is judgement day

I was settin on my bed

Holdin a loaded gun

Wantin to give up

And take my own life

Lookin down the barrel of the gun

I felt Jesus touch my hand

Sayin don't do this because

You have a purpose here

They still needed a chorus that would tie all of the verses together, and they decided to both think about it over the next few days. Then they would compare notes and see which one had the better chorus to use in the song. Austin was quiet at school the next few days as he thought about the right words to use in the song, and it made people wonder what he was thinkin about since he had gotten so quiet. Lane, on the other hand, couldn't focus with all the homework she was havin to do.

That Friday it was Jessica Roccha's birthday, and she was so excited to becomin a year older. That afternoon before her party the mail came, and in the mail was a birthday card from Austin. She was so excited to receive it and he even sent her five dollars with it. After she opened she had her mother read what the card said to her, and she smiled ear to ear as her mother read the last words of the card. Austin had signed the card love Austin which made Jessica's day, and she didn't really care about all the other presents that she got from family and friends.

When school started back on Monday after Thanksgivin, Jaelyn decided that she needed to talk to Austin because of all the stories that Mallory had been tellin the basketball team over the weekend at the tournament in Armstrong. She didn't know if Austin would even talk to her, but she had to know the truth for her own piece of mind. After Austin walked into the school and made his way to his locker, Jaelyn walked over as he put his book bag in his locker and got his books out for his first class, Jaelyn walked up a little scared and asked, "Is it true?"

"Is what true?" Austin replied, as he looked over at her shocked that she was talkin to him again.

"Are you sleepin with Mallory?"

"What?"

"Are you sleepin with Mallory?" Jaelyn said, as she slid over in front of him lookin him in the eye.

"Where did you hear that?"

"From the horse's mouth. She told the entire basketball all weekend at the basketball tournament."

"She lied to everyone." Austin said, crackin his boyish grin as he looked into her bright green eyes. "I haven't spent any time with her at all, since what happened at the bonfire party at Ryan's."

"But she talks to you durin school because I've seen her."

"I try to avoid her and only talk to her when I have to."

"You also talk to her in church."

"Yes, I know. But it's only when I have to."

"What have you been durin since September because you haven't gone to any of our friend's parties."

"I started a research project on my own." Austin explained, crackin his boyish grin.

"What kind of research project?"

"About a really cool guy."

"Oh, let me guess Elvis Presley."

"No, it's not about him."

"Then who is it about?"

"Someone I learned about over the summer. How's Remy?"

"How would I know?"

"I've heard from the horse's mouth that you're his girl."

"He's lyin to you."

"Well, you've gone to every dance with him."

"Only to make you jealous if you showed up to them." Jaelyn said, with a big smile on her face.

"Really?" Austin said, with a big smile and a laugh.

"I want to be with you, Austin Reid," Jaelyn said, crackin a grin as she put her arms around his neck.

"Remy, isn't goin to like that."

"I don't care." Jaelyn said, as she kissed him on the lips.

Three tables to the right of where Austin locker was Mallory was Watchin the conversation between Austin and Jaelyn, and she wasn't happy that the two of them were talkin to each other again. Not far from her Remy was talkin to a group of his friends when he noticed that Jaelyn was talkin to Austin again. Remy had told his friends in September that Jaelyn would be his girlfriend by the end of the year, but his plan wasn't goin as planned because Jaelyn wasn't wantin to spend any time with him at all. When his friends noticed that Jaelyn was talkin to Austin again they started to laugh, and told him that he didn't have any chance now that Jaelyn would be his girlfriend by the end of the year. Mallory and Remy both got really upset when they saw Austin and Jaelyn kissin each other in front of everyone in the cafeteria.

On Monday evenin Austin showed up to the girls' basketball game at the high school to support Jaelyn, and he was also there to support Jaedyn to Austin showed up early enough to watch the jv game and spend time with

257

Jaelyn before she played that night. Across the gym they could see Mallory watchin them where she wasn't playin in the game with the most upset look on her face. After the game was over. Austin was waitin in the gym for Jaelyn to give her a ride home since she rode with her sister back to high school with her sister. Mallory walked out of the girl's locker room and saw him standin by the doorway to walk out of the gym, so she walked over to where he was and said, "Your little game isn't goin to work, Austin Reid. I know that you want me…"

"Why don't you just give up." Austin said, as he turned around to look at her. "I will never be with you in that way."

"You say one thing, but your eyes tell me another."

"Just give up, Mallory. I don't want to be with you.."

Mallory leaned up kissin Austin on the lips and said, "Just give in and let me make you happy in ways that Jaelyn never can."

"Never goin to happen." Austin said, with a very serious look on his face.

"It will happen, Austin. Just wait and see.." Mallory said, as she put her hand on his chest as she started to walk away.

Just as she did that Jaelyn walked out of the girl's locker room talkin to her sister when she noticed Mallory walkin away from Austin. Jaedyn was just as shocked as Jaelyn was that Mallory would be stupid enough to talk to Austin knowin that Jaelyn could walk out of the locker room and catch her.

Jaelyn saw the smile on Austin's face and started to wonder if Austin had lied to her that mornin. As she and her sister walked up to where Austin was standin Jaelyn asked, "What was that all about?"

"She is still tryin to chase me." Austin said, crackin a big boyish grin. "But I told her I wouldn't be with her."

"You better have." Jaelyn said, as she gave him a kiss.

At the top of the ramp into the gym Mallory was watchin the conversation between Austin and Jaelyn. She was so upset that Austin wanted to be Jaelyn instead of her when she could make Austin happier than Jaelyn ever could. Jaedyn just watched the entire thing with a big smile on her face knowin that Mallory was seein just how much her sister and Austin were in love with each other.

259

Christmas seemed to come quickly that year, and on Christmas Eve
Austin's family gathered at Grandma Reid's house for Christmas dinner and
open Christmas presents. Austin and Lane went upstairs with their guitars to
brainstorm and hopefully finish the song that they were workin on. They
knew that the chorus had to be bright and happy with the verses bein so
dark. They played around with both major and minor chords still because
they still weren't happy with the chords they had picked out the last time the
two had gotten together. The two wanted to let the listener understand
that even though you might be goin through a dark time there was a light at
the end of the tunnel, and even if you didn't believe in God he would show
up to help you. Lettin you know that he was by your side showin you he was
the answer you needed. After brainstormin and throwin ideas off of each other
the two of them finally finished the song just before the family set down for
their meal. They asked their family to listen to and tell them what they thought
about it as the two strummed their guitars and sang they sang these words;

I was raised on the good book

Went to church every Sunday

Put on the righteous path

To the promise land

With the values of yesterday slipping away

Listenin to the preacher preach

Jesus is comin back someday

And so is judgement day

To be embraced in his arms

Cleansed by the blood of Jesus

My many sins washed away

Gettin a second chance to live

Now I'm a grown adult

I fight that fight of faith

But there was a time

When my believin was weak

One day I chose to give in to

The devil's temptations

Walkin right into darkness

And a life full of misery

Now I'm sittin on my bed

With a loaded gun

Wantin just to give up

And take my own life

Lookin down the gun barrel

I felt Jesus take my hand

Sayin don't do this because

You have purpose here

To be embraced in his arms

Cleansed by the blood of Jesus

My many sins washed away

Gettin a second chance to live

As the lightin flashed brightly

As the thunder rolled

As the rain fell down

I heard a rushin wind

I got down on my knees

Layin the gun down

Repentin of my sins

Askin God to forgive me

To be embraced in his arms

Cleansed by the blood of Jesus

My many sins washed away

Gettin a second chance to live

Their family was very surprised and shocked that Austin and Lane
could come up with a song that had such a message to it. Austin's
parents assumed that the two of them were just goin to sing other people's
song for the rest of their lives. Austin's father started to think that maybe both
Austin and Lane would really go far in their life because the two of them
worked so hard to get the song done. It was no secret in this town that
both Austin and Lane's parents thought that their younger siblins would
go farther than Austin and Lane because the two of them seemed to be more
interested in chasin after dreams that wouldn't really come true because a
person couldn't make a livin doin it. That's what Austin and Lane had heard
since the time they got their guitars from their uncle because they used him

as an example of why they wouldn't be able to make a livin doin it. Lane had turned her focus onto her writin, and worked on makin the best novel that she could. She was determined to show her family that she was goin to make somethin of herself no matter what they kept tellin her.

Christmas day arrived and that mornin after openin presents Austin decided to call Jessica Roccha and wish her a merry Christmas. The two talked on the phone for about thirty minutes because Jessica had to tell him what she had gotten for her birthday, and how happy she was to get a card from him. From the dinin room Austin's mother watched him, and wondered who he was talkin to since he and Jaelyn were goin really strong.. After Austin hung up the phone and started to walk back into the livin room with the rest of his family his mother asked, "Son, who were you talkin to?"

"Just a friend I made in Mississippi the last time I was there." Austin explained, with his boyish grin.

"Is this friend a person that Jaelyn has to worry about?"

"No, mom."

"What's this girl's name?"

"Her name is Jessica Roccha."

"Her name is Jessica." Austin's mother said, a little worried because of what he had just said,

"Don't worry, mom. She is only four years old, and still has a lot of growin up to do."

"She's four years old?"

"Yes, I met her while I was playin at the diner with the band this summer. Jessica is full of dynamite, and goin to be a handful when she grows up."

"Wait, was she one you got the letter from in the fall?"

"Yes, she was so taken with me that I told her I would write to her, and then she and her mother could write me back to tell me what was goin on in Saltillo."

"How cute.." Austin's mother said, with a big smile so happy with what her son was doin for that little girl. "I'm sure that the two of you will be best friends by the time she's grown up."

After walkin back into the livin room Austin's mother told his father what he was doin and how proud of him that she was. His father, on the other hand, was a little bit concerned because of the little girl's name, and he hoped that Austin wasn't goin down a rabbit hole that he wouldn't be able to get out of later. Sophia and Brandon just thought that their brother was bein the nice guy he'd always been. The two of thought their father was makin too much out of it just like he did with a lot of other things when it came to Austin.

New Year's Eve came and the church was havin a party to ring in nineteen ninety-nine. Although many churches didn't want you to drink, Austin's church had bought champagne for adults to drink at midnight. The preacher had also bought sparklin cider for the kids under twenty-one to drink, so that everyone would be included when midnight came. That night the fellowship hall was filled with lots of good food, and lots of people havin a good time. Austin and Jaelyn played a few games and hung out with their group of friends havin a good time. There was lots of laughter and smiles as everyone couldn't wait to start the new year. Across the room Mallory was watchin Austin and Jaelyn havin a good time together without a care in the world, and that made her jealous. Everything that Mallory ever wanted Jaelyn seemed to get first, and it had been that way since they had become friends back when Mallory was in the fourth grade. Around eleven thirty Reese, Hope, Peyton, Eileen, Maddie, and a few more of their friends sat down at the table beside

Mallory. The group started talkin and then Reese said, "I still can't believe that you tried to break those two up, Mallory."

"The two of them don't belong together." Mallory said, with an upset look on her face. "He would be better off with me."

"Do you really think that you will ever break those to up?" Peyton asked, wonderin what her answer would be.

"I think I will.."

"You don't have a chance in hell to do that." Maddie said, as she looked at her with a serious look.

"Why do you say that?"

"Austin and Jaelyn are serious about each other."

"I don't believe that." Mallory said, with a little grin. "When I flirt with him he always flirts back."

"But they are back together." Peyton said, puttin her two cents into the conversation.

"I know.."

"Austin loves Jaelyn.." Elieen said, as she looked over at Austin.

"Mallory, look at the two of them." Hope said, finally puttin her two cents into the conversation. "Does it look like he has any interest in you whatsoever?"

Across the room Austin and Jaelyn were sittin at a table all alone just havin a good time together. They were havin a conversation and laughin together. The two weren't worried about the world outside each other's eyes. For the people watchin them it seemed like the months they had spent apart had helped them learn just how important they were to each other. Many of the young couples in town looked up to Austin and Jaelyn were happy the two were back together again because it gave them hope for their own relationships.

As Austin looked deep into Jaelyn's green eyes he said, "I want to give you somethin."

"You do?" Jaelyn said, with a big smile and laugh wonderin what it could be since she had already got her Christmas present from him

"Yes, I do. I want to start this new year off with a bang."

"What have you done now?"

"I haven't done anything. I just feel that after what we have gone through this past year we need to start the year off on a good note."

"What have you done?" Jaelyn asked, as she looked into his ice blue eyes.

As Austin took off his class ring he said, "I want you to have my class ring, and I want to go study with you."

"You want to go study with me?"

"Yes, I do." Austin said, crackin his boyish grin. "And until I can buy a diamond ring to put on that left hand of yours my class ring will have to do."

"Wait? Are you sayin what I think you're sayin to me?"

"I think so."

"You're askin me to marry you right now?" Jaelyn replied, as a big smile came across her face.

"I am, but it's our secret because both of our parents would blow their tops if they knew that I asked you."

"Yes, they would."

"So it's just better if everyone think that we are just goin study." Austin said, as he handed her his class ring.

A few feet away the girls at the table with Mallory seen Austin take the ring off of his finger and hand it to Jaelyn. After the girls looked at each other for a few minutes the silence was broken when Peyton asked, "Did Austin just give Jaelyn his class ring?"

"I believe he did." Maddy said, with a big grin as she looked at Peyton.

"No, I don't think he did." Reese said, not believin what she just saw happen.

"Yes, he did." Eileen said, just as shocked as the rest of the girls at that table.

"Well, it looks like Jaelyn has taken Jessica's place in Austin's for good now." Hope said, knowin that for Austin to do that Jaelyn must be very important to him.

"I don't think that you have a chance now, Mallory." Reese said, with a big smile as she looked at Mallory.

"I'm not givin up on gettin Austin to go out with me." Mallory said, still determined that Austin would be her boyfriend.

"He just asked Jaelyn to study with him by givin her that ring, and that means the two of them are very serious about each other." Mary Ann said, puttin her two cents into the conversation, Mary Ann was a tall skinny girl

With long dark red hair and eyes that were very cautious. She had been a part of the group since junior high, and she was also a high achiever. She was home from Kentucky for the holiday season to visit with her family.

"I don't care, I'm still goin to chase after Austin until he is mine."

"You chasin him isn't goin to get you any closer to him." Eileen said, with a point. "You chase him he'll just get closer and closer to Jaelyn leavin you in the dust."

"I'm willin to take that chance." Mallory said, with a very determined look on her face lettin the girls know that she wasn't goin to quit.

The new year came with great expectations of what the year nineteen ninety-nine could have in store for everyone. In January of that year NASA's Mars Polar lander launched, Professional wrestler Jesse Ventura is sworn in as Governor of Minnesota. The sopranos debuts on HBO, the Clinton impeachment trial begins, Michael Jordan announces his second retirement prior to the start of the lockout NBA season, and super bowl XXXIII is played in Miami, Florida with Broncos beatin the Atlanta Falcons.

In Georgetown, Illinois news spread fast that Austin and Jaelyn were goin study, and upsettin a lot of the young girls in town. Lane was tryin to live her life in a positive mind every day, but was strugglin because every

272

time she turned around somethin tried to knock her down on the mat once
again. She was grateful that her grandma Sutton had become the cheerleader in her life, and lettin her know that she could do anything that she
set her mind to. Part of Grandma Sutton's drive was to make sure that her
kids and grandchildren finished school and would go on and make somethin
of themselves. She had gotten married at sixteen and didn't finish high
school. She became a mother at seventeen and was learnin to do all the
grown-up things while she was still a teenager. Grandma Sutton grew up in
a time when teenage kids did get married at an early age and started a
family not long after gettin married. Lane and Grandma Sutton would talk
for hours about things that Lane would never talk to her parents about.
She also talked to Grandma Reid about certain things that she wouldn't talk
to her parents or Grandma Sutton about.

As winter turned to spring Jaelyn along with everyone else in town
wondered why Austin had started lettin his hair grow out long because he
had always wanted to wear his hair short. His parents and even church people
didn't like that he was doin that because he wasn't followin church rules. The
church claimed to want everyone to come inside their church walls, but many
church people didn't want to hear about the road some people had to go down

273

to find Jesus. They wanted to hear that the person had found Jesus, but didn't want to hear about the x-rated parts of their story not realizin that the x- rated parts were the key of the person's testimony of how God had saved them for darkness.

Durin the Easter break durin the school year Lane went to Arkansas with her grandma and grandpa Sutton. It was a somber get together for the family because it was the first year without Gale, and she was the life of the party. Grandma Sutton, the rest of her sisters, and her mother put on their Easter hats like they did every year to see who could outdo the other one with the biggest hat. It just didn't feel right because Gale wasn't there to join in the fun. After the Easter celebration Lane and her grandparents went back to the hotel, Lane was bored out of her mind because her grandparents wanted to sleep so she couldn't do anything.

The next day they went down to Harrisburg to visit a cousin of Grandma Sutton's. They would drink coffee and talk for a few hours about the past and what was goin on in the present. Lane's extended family would always offer her a pop and somethin sweet to eat, and they would always tell how happy they were that she was takin care of her grandparents. On the way back to

274

Jonesboro Grandma Sutton would always want to go out to the cemetery that was between Jonesboro and Harrisburg because that's where her family members were buried. Grandpa Sutton pulled off the black top highway unto a red dirt road that you had to go very slowly on. About halfway down that road Lane saw what looked like a very old country church. The windows were knocked out of it, it needed a good paint job to bring back the white that was on it already, and the front door was boarded up. In front of the church there was two cars in the grass, and to Lane it just called for someone to restore it and have church services again. The three got to the cemetery and found where Grandma Sutton's family was buried at, and she always told Lane to be careful because blue racer snakes were always crawlin out there. She would tell the story of how her and her sister were out there visitin granny's grave when they started walkin away from it they saw a snake, and her sister ran and the snake chased after her for a brief moment. On the way back by the little church Lane got an idea of a song, so for the next few days the idea floated around in her as she thought about the right way to write it.

A week after gettin back from Arkansas Lane was listenin to Elvis's songs when the inspiration hit her to write the song that was floatin in her mind. She closed the book she was readin for one of her and picked up one of her many notebooks. As she opened the notebook she grabbed her favorite pencil and started writin down these words.

Many stories have I been told

A little church on an Arkansas red dirt road

People findin their love for singin

Cuttin their teeth on Amazin Grace

Preacher preachin about hell and temptation

Children settin on the edge of their seats

The Bible bein taught with such emotion

Adults loudly shoutin Amen

The church's heyday is gone

For a congregation it longs

To sing an upliftin spiritual song

To go back to a much simpler time

When people helped each other on a dime

Especially, if someone was in a bind

But the church's heyday is gone

Yes, it's heyday is gone

Times have changed but they're still the same

God and family are the most important

The church was long ago abandoned

But everyone is still welcome inside

Lit through the light by the window

A faded picture of Jesus on the wall

Under the layers of cobwebs and dust

On the pulpit lays a worn out Bible

The church's heyday is gone

For a congregation it longs

To sing an upliftin spiritual song

To go back to a much simpler time

When people helped each other on a dime

Especially, if someone was in a bind

But the church's heyday is gone

Yes, it's heyday is gone

Many souls were saved in that church

They in turn helped spread the gospel word

The church's heyday is gone

For a congregation it longs

Yes, it's heyday is gone

For what started out as a slow school year it sure went fast, and

before we all knew it prom time had come. All the teenage girls had gone

shoppin for their dresses, while the guys just thought bein in nice dress

pants and a nice shirt were enough. By this time Eloise and Waldo were

goin study, and he planned on goin to New York with her once she found

out if she was accepted into Julliard or not. Lee Ann and I were off and on

at this time because she said I was bein a selfish bastard when it came to wantin things my own way. I would also get very upset if she even talked to another guy because I was afraid that she would leave me for someone else who she thought was better. Beverly had been datin Tyler Rollins for about six months. He was a tall muscular man who played on the football team but also loved to sing and play guitar. Christine had been datin Daryl Somers for about four months, and the two seemed to get along. He was a tall bean pole of a guy who just adored her, and he was also on the football team. David played the steel guitar in his spare time and he loved country music. The girls had just about talked them into bein part of the band by the time school was almost out.

Up in Illinois Austin and Jaelyn were also gettin ready to go to his prom too. Jaelyn, Jaedyn, Mrs. Somerled, and her mother went to A store in Indianapolis to find the dresses that they wanted. Mrs. Somerled still couldn't believe that her youngest daughter was goin to the senior prom of her oldest daughter. She couldn't believe the two of them had grown up so fast right before her eyes. Across town Austin's mother couldn't believe that her first baby was goin to the last high school dance of his life. She had been cryin on and off all that afternoon. It was no surprise that his family followed Austin over to Jaelyn's house so they could get pictures of the two of them together. Austin just shook his head because he knew

That he would still have two years of taken pictures because he would be goin to Jaelyn's junior and senior proms with her. Once the picture taken started Jaelyn and Jaedyn seemed to just love the camera, but Austin and Jaedyn's date Mark were like cardboard cut outs. Jaedyn and Jaelyn had talked their parents into lettin them stay in the house that was one hundred yards away from the main house because Jaedyn was havin a little party after the prom. That Friday night Austin, Jaelyn, Jaedyn, and Mark dance their heart with all the other junior and seniors who went to the dance.

Around midnight a small group of Jaedyn's friends made their way to the small house not far from her parents' house. There were a few older friends there who brought some beer and wine coolers. Jaedyn and Jaelyn had set up the snacks before everyone else got there. Austin and Jaelyn hung out with the rest of the group for a few hours before they made their way to the back bedroom wantin to spend some time on their own.

As the moonlight shined through the window onto Jaelyn's face, she looked at Austin as he laid beside her on the bed and asked "So are you goin to leave town once you graduate?"

280

"I don't know." Austin said, as he looked over at her. "I haven't decided whether I am or not."

"You know that I'll be so lonely if you leave town."

As Austin looked deep into Jaelyn's green eyes he said, "I want to chase after my dreams, but the hold you have on me makes me want to stay."

"Good, because I want you to stay."

"You do?"

"Yes, I do." Jaelyn replied, as she set up on the bed. "My life will be so dull if you weren't here."

"I don't believe that."

"It's true.. I would probably sit at home and not go to any parties or hang out with any of my friends."

"You are a popular girl, so I don't believe that." Austin said, as he cracked his boyish grin.

"But with you not here to go to the parties with me I wouldn't have any fun." Jaelyn said, with a big smile and laugh.

"Well, I guess you are goin to have to convince me to stay in this little town and go to those parties with you."

"I think I can do that…" Jaelyn said, as she leaned over and kissed Austin on the lips.

"You are goin to have to try really hard because I'm leanin toward leavin town." Austin said, with a big grin as he kissed her.

The next mornin Jaedyn woke up as the sun shined through the windows in the livin room. She got up and looked around at all the teenagers sleepin on the livin room floor, but she didn't see Austin or Jaelyn anywhere. So she made her way down the hallway and started checkin the bedrooms because the two of them were told that no one could be in the bedrooms alone. When she got to the back bedroom at the end of the hall, she opened the door and found Jaelyn and Austin snuggled together in bed with Jaelyn wearin Austin's t-shirt. She knew what the two had done, and she wasn't goin to tell on them since she and Mark were doin the same thing.. So she knew that her and Jaelyn were at a pass because one tellin on the other would get both herself and her sister into trouble with their parents.

Down here in Mississippi our prom night was just as epic as Austin's was because of two guys gettin into a fight over a girl in the middle of After the dance was over we went back to Schlatter Farm to have a little party of our own. Needless to say, we didn't party as a group for a very long time because we went to our own little house partyin with just two people. I'm sure that if Hugo and Darlene knew what was goin on a at their farm they would be very upset. We all wondered why they never let anyone stay at the guest house that was closest to the main house. Beverly had told us that it was her great uncle's, and they had kept all of his belongins just as they were the day he died.

On May 23, 1999, Austin walked across the stage in Illinois graduatin from his high school, and down in Mississippi Eloise, Beverly, Lee Ann, Christine, me, and the rest of our class walked across the stage in our graduation. We were all so happy that we were finally out of school. But then most of us realized within two and a half months we would be headin back to school only this time it would be college. This time we had to get ourselves out of bed, and show up on time to class because our parents were treatin like us adults we had become.

Order Form.

Bell Sheep Publishing

214 E. 10th Street

Georgetown, Illinois

(217) 474-0410

Bonnie, Dexter, & Jesus

Paperback book……………………………$8.28___qty

Small Town Dreams; Beginnings

Paperback book……………………………$8.28___qty

Hardcover book……………………………$17.28__qty

Shipping

1-10 books………………………………$5.28

10-20 books……………………………$9.28

20 or more………………………………$15.28

Qty_____

Subtotal_____

Shipping_____

Total_____

www.ingramcontent.com/pod-product-compliance
Lightning Source LLC
Chambersburg PA
CBHW021218260626
47172CB00002B/485